John Alexander Harvie-Brown

The Wonderful Trout

John Alexander Harvie-Brown

The Wonderful Trout

ISBN/EAN: 9783744791236

Printed in Europe, USA, Canada, Australia, Japan

Cover: Foto ©Andreas Hilbeck / pixelio.de

More available books at **www.hansebooks.com**

THE
WONDERFUL TROUT

BY

J. A. HARVIE-BROWN

'Thus does the salmon vault.'
DRYDEN.

EDINBURGH : DAVID DOUGLAS
10 CASTLE STREET
1898

PREFACE

In all scientific endeavour and elaboration, those who strain after perfection, and put off that hour when they hope to get beyond criticism, only stand in their own light and in the light of real discovery.

By the time they decide (*i.e.* if they ever do) to publish the results of many years' experience, it may be then they only do so and find there is 'nothing new under the sun.' Such delay is more likely to end in disappointment and chagrin than if they published prematurely. It is the *embryo of a new idea* which adds to future knowledge, because it sets many a-thinking years before the thought-wave would be otherwise started. If Darwin had more elaborated before publishing, Wallace might have outstripped him.

And if he had, would *scientia* have been better forwarded than it is now ? This straining after perfection is a great loss to science, though we do not advocate the other extreme of *unripe*, unthought-out data. The happy medium, of course, is hard to hit.

This may seem a pretentious Preface to a '*littel worke*,' but we hope there may appear in it at least a germ of sensibility.

DUNIPACE, LARBERT,
  28th Sept. 1898.

CONTENTS

I

INTRODUCTORY

II

DEPRECATORY

III

SIZE AND AGE OF TROUT

IV

ANGLING REQUISITES

V

DEFENCE OF UP-STREAM FISHING

VI

FLIES

VII

ON TROUTING WITH THE FLY—THE PRACTICE

VIII

THE CAPTURE

IX

WORM IN CLEAR WATER

X

WEATHERS AND ELECTRICAL DISTURBANCES

XI

FOOD-SUPPLIES AND RELEVANT MATTERS

XII

TROUTING WITH OTHER DEVICES—CLOSE TIMES
AND POACHING

XIII

CLOSE TIMES FOR TROUT

XIV

NOTIONS, NOTES, AND ODDS AND ENDS

I

INTRODUCTORY

WITH most of Stewart's practice and the outcome of his teaching as a north country angler we agree, because, during all our novitiate and practice, and all the more strongly of later years (after many seasons mostly devoted to salmon-fishing), we have ever been enthusiastically an upholder of the up-stream method of angling for trout, and that almost from the first time we perused Stewart's invaluable treatise. As a boy we had practised it, and again as a 'grown-up.'

Since then we have read and studied every succeeding edition and compared them, noting the changes and slight alterations in the texts of each, which in several cases are modifications of the originals, according as the seasons may have altered, or as trout have become more educated (or

A

frightened), and 'fisherfolk' have become more abundant, and anglers—good and bad —have increased in number. As we believe, the worst enemy the truly scientific angler has lies in the troops of unscientific anglers who thresh every stream as with a flail, and cast their long shadows over the thin waters.

In our present volume, and all during our practice, we have every season taken up Stewart's points; and we have patiently endeavoured, day by day, to prove their correctness or discover their imperfections. We have also, by careful analyses of re- peated experiences and by experiments, as conscientiously tried to *give reasons* for many, if not for all, of Stewart's conclu- sions, and his well-proved array of facts. Examples of this may be found under the headings of 'Temperatures of Air and Water,' 'Descriptions of Weather,' 'State of Water'; and the Tables, showing the averages of various conditions and circum- stances—in fact, the *raison d'être* of his whole arguments and practice.

Where we find, as we believe, reasons to differ, or where changes in conditions have supervened since Stewart wrote, causing changes which he did not, and most likely could not, foresee, we have tried to give reasons as they occurred to us that came within our belief and practice.

Pure theory will be kept out so far as possible, though we may claim that certain deductions present themselves. But 'Theories and Notes and Notions' may have a chapter to themselves.

And now, once for all, let it be understood at this outset, we are not offering a treatise on trout-fishing generally, but these pages refer to river-fishing only. Stewart in his first Preface says: 'The information received (from others) we have thoroughly tested before admitting it.' In like manner we claim to have done the same, at least during the last eight or nine years' trout-fishing out of a total experience of, alas! close upon forty years' actual angling for trout and salmon—for we began under tuition, before any 'standards' had to be 'passed'; so, if the education was slower, possibly it may prove more stable and lasting.

Stewart in his Preface to the Fourth

Edition, whilst acknowledging the favourable reception of previous editions by the
press and by many eager and interested
pupils, still points out (p. x) that 'darkness rather than light is the deliberate
choice of the million,' and *this* fact we hope
to bring out more emphatically. Notwithstanding the aforesaid reception, the average
local angler of to-day (A.D. 1898) does not
fish up-stream in any state, on any stage of
water, upon at least nine-tenths of the rivers,
large or small, of Scotland.

We do not desire to appear even to
assume a higher standard of authority than
we honestly believe we possess. We humbly
think, after these many years, that we
cannot compete with hundreds of other
anglers, old and young (young especially!),
whose opportunities and experiences, energies
and abilities, have very likely been extended
over double or treble or ten times the areas
that ours have. What we try to aim at is
to get a large body of fisherfolk to give
up that terrible practice of 'flailing down-
stream' under all conditions of flood and
drought, thereby frightening all the decent-

sized fish for fifty yards before them, and take to the more scientific practice now so long advocated by up-stream anglers. We lay the principal blame of deterioration of well-stocked rivers upon this suicidal practice.

Angling (scientific angling, and even—as all know—even the coarsest forms of the sport) becomes a *passion* to any one who has tasted its delights and disappointments, its concomitant pleasures and regrets, and the charms associated with the 'Contemplative Man's Recreation.'

II

DEPRECATORY

'Subsequent experience has convinced us, not
only as good, but better, *sport* may be had in
clear water than in coloured.'—[*P. A.* Preface,
p. xii, 4th Ed.]

FOR many years past we have refused to
'flail' with a two-handed rod from the bank
of a flooded water under conditions such as
the following. But there is, we believe, a
large majority of local anglers, and also of
itinerant anglers, whose chief object is to go
out and kill something, and whose apprecia-
tion of that little word yclept 'sport' con-
sists in the size of their 'take,' whether the
fish be in good condition or not. 'Sport'
it no doubt is, but only, we maintain, in a
degree far below that obtained under the
different conditions we advocate. We do

6

not ourselves enjoy 'sport' under the following circumstances :—

(*a*) When, early in the season, trout are not in 'decent' or even 'wonderful condition for the time of year,' and are still half starving, and only beginning to recuperate, after the severe conditions of their natural winter existence. Nor at such times as the fishing papers are full of 'big, record baskets.'[1] [Remember we speak of *river*-angling.]

(*b*) When, in early April, the sky is dark and gloomy, or when only fitful flares of sunlight intervene. When the rivers run full and dark or inky black from combined effects of sky and matter in suspension. Sometimes these conditions are combined with high gales of north and north-east winds.

(*c*) When the temperature of the water is vastly below that of the air, or when both the temperatures of air and water are below

[1] We associate many of these records, in a whimsical sense, with an ancient rhyme which began—'Fe Fi Fo Fum,' etc.—but some others certainly issue from a few informed sources also which are situate north of the Borders and north of the Grampians. We trust none of our 'not-guilty' English or other friends will feel hurt at the allusion.

a certain point, about which we will have
more to say further on.

In early spring it is not always on
warm days, with *slowly heating* water,
that the biggest hatch-off of fly-food
takes place. Flotillas of March Browns
and Early Duns are most often witnessed when the air is colder than the
water, *i.e.* if both are above the certain
point on the thermometer scale. A bright,
warm blink of sun occurring about the time
of the hatch-off of fly—say 10.30 to 11 or
12 noon—will certainly assist the hatch-off.
Not much before the time when snow-water
has cleared away do larvæ rise to the surface
and become fly-food.

In the above statements it will be seen we
remove some portion of the emphasis which
Stewart puts upon the *state of the weather* (*v.*
p. 122) as the only, or principal, factor in the
birth of water-insect life. By long experience
we have come to the conclusion that the rising
of trout depends less upon the coldness or
warmth of the atmosphere separately than
upon the comparative temperatures ruling
between air and water; and that if water be

greatly lower in temperature than the air, trout
do not rise well. When both temperatures are
too low they do not rise well. But if the temperatures are nearly equal, above about 53°
to 55°, they often do rise well; and especially
in summer, if the temperature of the air be
cooler than that of the water, they rise best.
Often in a backward spring the water and
the air become colder as the day advances
instead of warmer, as we have repeatedly
proved, and this is most fatal to the hatching
off of water insects. A continuation of high
floods, and dark skies, and dark waters, with
these low temperatures, sum up the worst
circumstances that can befall the spring or
early summer angler, and, in consequence,
the trout fail to get into their best condition
from the absence of winged insect food.
Such a season was 1898, at least upon the
less aerated reaches of our rivers. Under the
above conditions, as we have said, we refuse to
' flail.' We often prefer to sit still when other
anglers are—in the words of Stewart—' ex-
ercising unlimited patience ' (*op. cit.* p. 2). For
hours together we have in vain watched a
long, lovely reach of water, to detect the

motion of a fin, the ring, or, as an old mentor
of our own youth used to call it, ' No' even
the mairk o' a troot.' Nor is it only that we
have watched such a reach, but we have over
and over again fished it; and if we caught
some trout, they were oftener than not
smaller than our river average, or if large, in
poor condition, ' without ' (so to speak) ' a
kick in them.' We have fished innumerable
times under precisely similar and recorded
conditions, and have stopped in the middle
of killing trout, after putting back many a
trout which, had his weight corresponded
with his measurements, would have weighed
over the lb. (See Table at p. 137.)

To reiterate in other paraphrase, we seldom
care to ' flail ' and ' chuck and chance it ' with
a two-handed rod or ' pole ' from the bank of
a flooded or high-coloured water in early
spring (nor, indeed, at any season) when the
trout are not in full condition, on a dark,
gloomy, sunless day, and the temperatures
do not improve as the day advances; when
the water looks black as ink; when the
surface of a pet glide or ripply reach bears
the colour of a new pair of patent leather

boots or a Lincoln and Bennett brushed the
wrong way, or when one has to use 'flees
that are not flies,' as big as a 'bumble-bee'
or the historical 'bee in the bonnet.' And if
we do, and bring the bigger trout home, we do
not eat them—unless, like the man with the
bad egg, we try to 'pick out the best bits.'
We have known the same experiences when
the so-called 'finnocks,' caught by the sack-
ful, basketful, or trayful in early spring in our
estuarial waters, have been and constantly
are thrown out to the pigs. Just as soon
'shoot a hen pheasant on Sunday morn; on
a midsummer day, in standing corn.' Says
Stewart: 'It is unsportsmanlike in the
highest degree to kill fish that are of no
use,' and 'they are never in condition till
they get abundance of insect food' (*op. cit.*
pp. 22, 23).

The question of 'butchery' spoken of by
Stewart, and his estimates of possibilities
in the way of large baskets, comes up. If
the 'sport' of angling lies in the capture of
fish, it seems evident that the more fish the
better sport. We agree with this, but we
reserve the opinion, that such is not 'sport'

unless the fish are fit for human food afterwards.   In Stewart's estimates of sport he
quotes 'between May and October.' We are
inclined to quote between May and the end
of September (for Brown Trout) or, on a few
early streams, from, say, the 15th April to
the end of July, as the true fishing season
for Brown Trout in streams of Scotland.
September only in some streams (and lochs,
of course).

As to the quantities mentioned in his
famous statements — altered in the later
editions—these were written long ago, when
'fisherfolk' and anglers were much scarcer,
and these need not be now used in evidence
nor argument except as items of antiquarian
interest and in a comparison of then and now.
Tempora mutantur et mutamur in illis.
But we incline to believe and agree with
Stewart when he writes, 'Angling is much
better *sport* now than it was fifty years ago '
(pp. 31, 32), and we agree with his reasons.
But we *do* hold, it is hard indeed to see
true 'sport' spoiled by cubic-length shadows
of men, and sixteen-foot poles, thrown all
over the water by the 'down-streamers,' when

the sky is clear, the river low, the sun high overhead in the blue, and, as likely as not, *behind them*! Thus three or four miles of water capable of supplying sport to three or four scientific anglers are, day after day, season after season, *destroyed* upon many reaches by *one man* and *a pole*.

III

SIZE AND AGE OF TROUT

STEWART in his great treatise evidently refers
with most experience and knowledge to his
southern or border streams. This becomes
evident when he speaks in a general way of
the size of trout being dependent upon the
size of rivers and feeding qualities. He
instances some more northern rivers as examples of streams where 'trout are neither
numerous nor large' (*v.* p. 19). Thus he
instances Spey and *most* Highland streams.
He is unfortunate in his selection of a type
in Spey. Spey holds very large trout over
all its reaches, and on its upper beats yields
excellent trout-fishing in the season. In
another place he assigns a curious reason
for the scarcity of trout in certain rivers.
He says: 'Small rivers produce more trout

14

in proportion to their size than large ones, as a large river has not so much bed in proportion to its size. It is principally the bed of a river which yields the insects and other food upon which trout live.' There is undoubted truth in the remarks; but insufficient attention appears to have been given to the great exceptions, if such indeed they are. Thus Spey, Tay, Tummel, Don, Deveron, Inver, and even his own Tweed; do these not class among larger rivers, and do they not claim rank amongst our best trouting streams? Again he says: 'Trout are seldom so numerous in rivers where salmon-par abound; are rarely such good trouting streams as those where there are none, the small fish consuming a large proportion of the food of the river.' We fail to reconcile our own experiences with this latter statement, and again instance the same rivers mentioned above, which are not only large rivers, but also rivers 'infested with par.' [Salmon men! don't look askance at the expression. *We* are speaking of trout. If salmon-fry eat much of the food, trout and salmon kelts eat much of the fry.]

Now, as regards the age of trout, possibly—
indeed, almost certainly—at the time Stewart
wrote, there were not so many opportunities
of proving the ages of trout (v. p. 19); and
subsequent experiments and experiences
both of our own hatcheries, and our own
streams (and lochs and ponds), and even
more so of such as have been instituted in
some of our colonies at the Antipodes and
elsewhere, tell us much more than Stewart
then knew. We will only instance a few
examples known in our own experience or
obtained from what we consider thoroughly
reliable sources, e.g.—

A trout nineteen years in confinement was
seen by us in 1892. It was confined in a
drain close to the then-gamekeeper's house
on Castle Grant estates, near Grantown.
This fish was taken originally from Loch-an-
Dorb, along with others, and all except this
one were conveyed to the ponds at Cullen
House. This one had been overlooked and
came back in the carrier-tin. Mr. Templeton, the keeper—of long years' service in the
Seafield family—had kept and fed it for nearly
twenty years, until it became so tame as to

feed out of his own and even strangers' hands.
The apparent size of the trout was about
thirteen inches or more, and weight at somewhat over the pound when we saw it. Mr.
Templeton died in July 1892, about one
month after we paid him a visit.

Again, in the Howietoun ponds, as we
were (alas!), and are, informed on the best of
authorities, the age of trout—or rather, we
should say, the age of growth in trout—there
does not usually exceed from five to seven
years, but the artificial conditions must be
considered. Of the age and growth of trout
transplanted we have had various experiences, both *from* natural *to* natural sources
and depositories, from artificial to artificial,
and from artificial to natural. Of the first,
viz. in several lochs and streams of Assynt,
we found the growth rapid under the new
natural conditions, but in many cases we
found the deterioration afterwards equally
rapid. That meant *aged fish*, perhaps not
larger than six to the pound when introduced,
feeding up fast in muscular development,
but, likely as not, overtaxing their constitu-
tions before the time when their spawning

season arrived, and then rapid decadence. Of this subject we may have more to say under a later chapter, and when we come to speak more pointedly of food supplies.[1]

New revelations have been made as regards the life-history of the eel in salt water, since this part of our writing was done.[2] We believe that our Salmon Commissioners have almost as much to learn as regards the life-history of our migratory fish in salt water; and that quite as interesting, and even startling, results may yet be revealed.

[1] Refer to Stewart's notes :—pp. 21-23, Preservation and conservation ; p. 24, Causes of diminution of trout in many streams ; p. 25, Effects of drainage—sheep and cattle ; p. 21, Elvers, and fly-food, and larvæ, and condition ; p. 32, Causes of deterioration, and the averages of different streams.

[2] International Zoological Congress, at Cambridge, August 1898, q.v.

IV

ANGLING REQUISITES

On this subject we have not much to say. The best advice we can give is to buy periodically, and bind up sets every few years, of as many of our best tackle-makers' catalogues as will make up a handy portable volume of reference, and, as experience may teach you, purchase therefrom.

Only where we differ from Stewart, or where later improvements unknown in his day give occasion, shall we have anything to say, and then only where we have personally used these more important later improvements.

The subject of the choice of a rod need not be dilated upon. Indeed this seems to us not to be a true subject for fair or useful discussion in a book, and should be reserved for personal and individual selection and practice. 'What is one man's food is often another man's poison.' Custom, strength of wrist, delicacy of touch and manipulation must rule the style of rod and tackle used. It seems to us that much of what Stewart complained of, viz. 'excessive pliability of rods made in Edinburgh,' has long since been obviated both there and by other makers, whether makers famed for their greenheart trout-rods or makers famed for their split-cane rods, the latter either *in toto* or in combinations. We have not hitherto had any direct experience of steel-centred rods. Split-cane rods, such as now can be obtained—*only, however, from the best makers*—were not known at the time Stewart wrote his complaint, nor were greenheart rods so beautifully balanced and presented as is now the case. Of joints, ferrules, bayonet-slots, and outside and inside screws and whippings, much depends upon the idiosyncrasy of the individual, not to speak of his actual experiences. We ourselves know what we *like* best of such as we have used, and, it is to be expected, so should

other people. The advantages of thin gut
(and good) need not be rewritten, nor its
importance again be belauded. But our
belief may be expressed that for Scottish
streams the fine, clear, round gut (undrawn)
for fine fishing is the best, and a tapered
cast, though two feet shorter, is better than
a long cast made up of long lengths of finest
gut only. We see some anglers using warm
water to steep their gut and flies in. We
ourselves prefer cold. Lastly, we fully
re-echo Stewart's concluding sentences of
chapter iii. p. 54. But of flies we will have
more to say further on.

V

DEFENCE OF UP-STREAM ANGLING

Certainly we look upon fly-fishing for trout, under sporting conditions, as the acme of an angler's pleasure. But not under the conditions we have already pointed out. Nevertheless there are the *seasons*—those for fly-fishing as a scientific recreation, and others where fly-fishing is supplanted by the almost equally fascinating ' worm-fishing in clear water.' Regarding these seasons we need not enlarge. They may, and do, vary on rivers large and small, or according to lateness or earliness, altitudes and local conditions, but the *best times* for either and for both have been repeatedly and correctly pointed out.

Undoubtedly fly-fishing in low, clear water is ' beyond compare the most difficult of all the branches of the angler's art, and should

22

therefore rank highest as "sport."'   So says
Stewart, and *he is right!*

WHEN SHALL WE GO A-FISHING?

I

No bumble-bees are humming,
No willow catkins coming,
And the river's high and banked by cauld snaw-bree.
There's nae liltin' o' the thrushes,
There's nae cooin' o' the cushies,
And nae wadin' i' the watter tull the knee.

II

For it's cauld, cauld, cauld upon the lea ;
There's nae growth atween the upland and the sea,
For there's snaw ahint the dykes,
There's a seugh amang the sykes,
And it's jist aboot as cauld as it can be.

III

Will *we* then gang a-fishin',
Whan the winter snaws are rinnin',
And the troots are lang and lank as they can be ?—
Na ! we will gang a-fishin'
When the poplar-trees are blushin',
And the bumble-bee is hummin' ower the lea.

IV

For we prefer troot-fishin'
Whan the troots are in condition,
And we're wadin' i' the watter tull the knee ;
For it is o' nae avail
Tull gang *fushin'* wi' a flail—
As weel gang for *sillocks*[1] in the sea !

---

[1] Podlies.

What more lovely than in a clear, low 'stickle,' below where tiny streamlets meet, perhaps a foot in depth, or it may well be not more than six inches, than to take out by dexterous angling with the fly and a tapered line, not more than fifteen feet from top of rod in length, from six to eight or more three-to-the-pound trout, and perhaps a pounder as well, and this when the sky is blazing blue without a cloud! And when this 'stickle' is not more than twenty yards in length, terminating in the big pool below —the hold of every trout that is feeding on the shallow—what more delightful than to stalk its lower tail-race, work it up foot by foot, pull each successive capture down into the pool, and kill each on the channel below, disturbing naught above! Then, when you have done with it, what more astonishing, it may be to an onlooker, to observe the water in the centre of the stream, as you cross over to another similar summer 'stickle,' does not take you so deep as the top of an ordinary ankle-boot ? [1]

[1] An excellent article upon the practice of this art— *Trout-Fishing in Rapid Streams*—will be found in a

Undoubtedly also, next to this method
ranks that of the scientific worm-fisher under
almost precisely similar conditions of sky
and water, but at a somewhat later season,
i.e. later in the summer. The second naturally takes the place of the first when the
right season arrives. Fly-food is not taken
by trout after the proper fly-season ends
nearly to the same extent, nor with the
same eagerness; and during the daytime, at
least, the best-conditioned trout and the
largest are sure to come at the worm if
properly presented under the correct conditions of good angling and up-stream wind
and propitious weather, of which we will
have more to say.

But, avaunt! Observe a long exciseman [1]

---

volume with that title, by H. C. Cutcliffe, p. 110 *et seq.*
Excellent instructions also are to be found in *How to
Catch Trout* (D. Douglas, 1888), and in *Fly-Fishing for
Salmon, Trout, and Grayling,* by Edward Hamilton, M.D.,
1884. Also, some wise truths can be culled from Pritt's
Introduction to his *North Country Flies* (1886).

[1] 'Remember the black beetles, horrid things, and be
sure to well sprinkle the river-banks with "Keating's
Powder," the unrivalled killer of fleas, beetles, moths.
Harmless to animals. Sold only in tins, 3d., 6d., and
1s. each.'

or some local angler who 'prefers the darkness rather than the light,' as he comes
striding down the river's brink, a pole over
his shoulder, or waving like a poplar in a
gale over the devoted stream; throwing his
coil far down before him, and covering
perhaps four miles of river-bank and acres
of water, not more than a foot or eighteen
inches in depth, which, however, hold trout
it is just about able to conceal.

Evening comes, and he comes back to
'mine inn' a sadder, perhaps, but often a no
wiser man.   He complains bitterly of a
'bothering up-stream wind.'   He produces
(or not, as he pleases) a few par and an odd
trout not much bigger than gudgeon, which,
with a backward wave of his sixteen-footer,
he had chucked into the nearest road of the
adjoining parish.   He never thinks of com-
plaining of his 'cubits' or his 'pole,' or the
long shadows cast over four miles of water
which he has covered *with his line*; nor does
he dream of apologising to other anglers—
who would have been content to fish *correctly*
any one half-mile or mile of the same, and
have brought in, say, seven or eight pounds

of trout—as having destroyed the reach for
that day and probably for several.

As Stewart says, 'He plies his lures to
the terror and alarm of almost every trout
in the water.' That man, or *such like him*,
should only thrust his obnoxious presence
on the stream-side when the trout are roving
in a coloured water, or on an early April day
when the fish are in condition *good enough
for him.* He can then enjoy himself
according to his lights, and not interfere so
much with true 'sport.' Such fishing does
far more to make trout shy and cautious
than any amount of scientific angling.

Stewart in the days of his practice and
writing believed 'that ninety-nine out of
every hundred fishers fished *down*, and never
thought of attributing their want of success
to their doing so.' And at that time Stewart
(*i.e.* about 1857) had 'only met one or two
amateurs and a few professionals who fished
up-stream.' In our own angling travels we
still find in A.D. 1896, and up to the present
date, 'darkness rather than light is the
deliberate choice' of by far the largest
number of (shall we say illiterate ?) fishermen.

But we have even heard the system of down-stream fishing defended by men who were not only educated men, but by some who rank high as scientific thinkers, and whose abilities as anglers are often praised. It seems strange—to us at least—to hear the reasons they give. How, for instance, can they affirm that 'more water is covered in down-stream fishing than in up-stream fishing'? We admit the fact, but it is covered by the line, not by the flies, and the mileage is certainly, as we have shown, longer. In other words, the river-bank is covered by strides and the water by shadows, and clear against the sky behind 'the man with the pole' is silhouetted, to the horror of every trout within fifty yards. The streams are 'covered' by hops, skips, and jumps, and unnatural jerks of an insect imitation. A salmon-fisher must reach the lie of the fish, and then *hang* his lure over it if he expects to 'bring him up,' and that by casting down-stream. But a trout-fisher, by 'covering' a large extent of water 'fine and far off,' does so with his line, not his flies, and passes over feeding fish, frightens many—ten times more

than are caught—*i.e.* if he fishes in *low, clear*
water, where the up-stream angler makes his
baskets. On a half-flooded or amber water
it may be well to fish *across* the stream,
standing, however, well back from the verge,
and then allow your three flies—or four
are permissible at such times — to drift
down a few yards or feet, and then cast
again; and often good baskets are thus
made, but it is not good enough in a low,
thin water. 'Fine and far off' seems to us
an exploded phantasy, so far at least as
Scottish streams are spoken of. We write
of Scottish sport. Possibly in the chalk
streams of Hampshire, with the dry or floating fly, 'fine and far off' is still a necessity.
In this style of angling we have, we confess,
only served a *novitiate.* We would for
Scottish sport substitute the advice, 'In
water clear, cast fine and near,' *up-stream*, or
up and across, unless occasionally when it is
desirable to reach a rising fish, across, or
under the opposite bank, or properly to hang
a fly in a far-off eddy or swirl by changing
your position.

And now a few words about 'striking one's

fish.' As Stewart points out, in angling down-stream, 'if a trout rises and an angler "strikes" he runs the risk of pulling the flies straight out of its mouth, whereas in fishing up, its back is to him and he has every chance of bringing the hook into contact with its jaws' (*v.* p. 65). Later we will speak of the colour of sky and cloud as a factor in what is called 'short-rising' of trout (and salmon); but meanwhile, apart from these conditions, causes—proofs, we believe—can be found in a fault in the practice as pointed out by Stewart.

Either in up- or down-stream fishing the angler 'strikes,' as it is usually termed, or *gently raises his hand.* Some 'strike from the reel,' and to accommodate this class of anglers the makers of the 'Requisites' will now meet him half-way. Except on rare occasions we look upon this 'striking from the reel' as only a clumsy excuse for too excitable nerves and want of coolness and self-possession. The advice by an onlooker would probably be, if he wished to increase the excitable condition of the angler, 'Don't get excited: keep cool. Take a drink, and you will have less short rising.' (The reply might probably be 'Darn!' or something stronger.)

The seemlier way we believe to be a gentle raising of the hand, or what may be described as the 'turning of a key in the well-oiled lock of a door.'[1] This is easy in the case of up-stream fishing with a short, taut line between rod-top and tail-fly, but the more difficult the longer the line used, and when a big slack of the line has to be recovered.

The other advantages of fishing up are all detailed by Stewart. Undoubtedly up-stream fishing is harder exercise than is down-stream fishing, and we will endeavour to illustrate this. On one occasion in which we were ourselves fishing up along with an angling friend, and we were passing one another, taking hundred-yards reaches time about. The one counted the other's casts, timing with a stop-watch, and repeated the

[1] We wrote this description at the time, either not knowing that it was so written before, or forgetting that we had read it (see Younger's *River Angling*, 2nd edit., 1864, p. 127). Anyway, we believe in the description as perhaps as accurate a one as can be found anywhere in angling literature.

experiment over and over again to test its accuracy. The conclusion was arrived at that the one who was angling made fifteen casts in one minute. He who was fishing thus was not at the time aware of the presence behind him of his friend. Therefore if a day's fishing be put down at, say, six hours (we are usually content with much less), fifteen a minute would give 5400 casts per diem. By deducting one hour for lunch and other intervals—' fankles,' pipes, and landing and netting one's fish—that figure would be reduced to 4500 casts. As Stewart tells us, the alighting of the fly is the most deadly in the whole cast, therefore the oftener it is repeated the better.[1]   Later on, when we intend to speak of the actual process and practice, and describe the fishing-up of a reach or pool or stream, we may make the reason of such frequent casting more distinct. Meanwhile let us ask the question : How many casts will the down-stream fisher make per hour, or per minute, when covering four miles of bank and acres of water

---

[1] But we do not agree in this altogether with Stewart (see further on).

with his line. We leave the question to be answered by the 'down-streamer.' The hard work in 'down-streaming' comes in, not for the arms, and eyes, and mind, but in the cubits, and the strides, and mileage, and weight of the pole.

It is seldom needful to use a longer line than one and a half times the length of the rod—*i.e. if wading up*; nor a longer rod than a single-handed twelve-foot rod. Yet we have seen otherwise good up-stream anglers using too long a line, which ought to become evident to themselves, if they observed the continuous loss of time by 'fankling' and subsequent mismanagement at the time of a rise of fish—all hurry and little speed, curses not loud but deep, and sometimes accompanied by frantic gestures. 'The nearer we are to our flies the better we can use them, and the greater the chance of hooking' (p. 107).

But on large, heavy, and rapid rivers, such as the Spey, where the current is strong—as, for instance, on the Aberlour water and Rothes, the former of which we are acquainted with as a salmon-fisher—it is 'most impossible' to wade up against the stream, and fishing down is imperative. There, in the spring months, local and other anglers wade in long waders, or fish from the bank for trout with long rods and big flies, with 'flies that are not flies,' any more than a 'Spey Dog' or a 'Jock Scott' or a 'Durham Ranger' is a fly. These are thrown far out into the deep streams, and worked just like a salmon fly, and are taken by large and heavy trout. But as a rule they are 'some saft i' the fish' (*i.e.* somewhat soft in the flesh), and rather 'woolly' on the table.[1] Such, however, are better killed. Similar fishing may be had on the large rivers like Tay and Tummel, where up-stream angling would be imposs- ible or too fatiguing. Such afford the best chances to the adept down-streamer or the man of cubits and a pole. We call it 'salmon- fishing for trout.' Like 'Old Lloyd' of Scandinavian fame, he may wade up to his navel, and whenever he feels tired could sit down on a stone at the bottom ! He would

---

[1] Whimsically, about the same difference in flavour as there is between Highland black-faced mutton five years old, and Cheviot stock mutton one and a half years old !

then do other anglers no harm, nor disturb the fish 'any more, whateffer!'

There is, however, one good reason for fishing down when the river is high and flooded, and when too deep to wade with comfort. At such times the trout are more scattered, unless in certain eddies or close to the banks, and then the *man* and *the pole* has more right on his side to fish down and cover more *miles* and *acres*. But the very proof of this being so must surely show to the same individual that when the river 'falls in' to normal states of condition, when 'wadin' to the knee' is necessary for concealment, when the trout are more circumscribed of necessity by the contracting of the channel and clearing of the shallows, surely the conditions are reversed! Certainly, in flooded or high conditions of water, fishing down (and walking down) covers more water with the line and miles of the bank, and it becomes necessary to do this to make a good basket. But as certainly it is unnecessary when the river becomes low and clear.

Fishing long in one place.—It is against

precedent and usual practice to persist too
long over one spot, or attempt to do what
some people advocate, 'bully a fish into
rising.' But all rules seemingly have their
exceptions, and when such occur the reasons
are often not far to seek. Instance :—Ob-
serving a small space of water, not larger
than the crown of a hat, at the edge of a
swift current of water, where a big fellow
was steadily feeding ('rising to himself,' as
expressed in the Highlands), we fished up
to him, then across to him, then down to
him, *i.e.* in the direction of the stream,
which ran swiftly past this side eddy. At
last the fly—a 'Greenwell's Glory'—came to
him—*as he would wish to be done by*; and
he took it with a rapid, hungry rush, and
we had him—*as we would be done by.* At
least twenty casts we had put over him as
he 'bobbit aboot wi' a wonderful snout, and
cockit his tail oot o' favour' (Stoddart).
Many such experiences we have had. The
lesson taught is: Try till you get the fly to
hang over him correctly; shift your position
of attack; he believes a swarm of flies are
coming down; he is *keen* to respond; treat

him fairly and he'll curtsy to you, though at times he may only play 'snooks' at you.

Another occasion for persistent fishing and oft-repeated casting over the same water has been advocated by a south country angler or anglers—'The Marquess of Granby and others'—in *The Fur, Feather, and Fin* series, 1898, *q.v.* p. 28.

A lovely little slip, as it appears to us *northern anglers*, comes in in the words 'even when fishing up-stream,' and the following remarks about the 'parson and the grey hackle-fly,' a 'small partridge hackle' (p. 29), positively make us 'chuckle,' in common, I presume, with other north country anglers.

The occasion they mention is that of 'tailing' of fish, which we speak of under 'Food-supplies,' *infra*; and we are perfectly 'at one' with them when they recommend 'hackle-flies' as the most useful under such conditions. We could add another 'tip,' but do not feel inclined to commit ourselves, as it is only very lately we have tried it, both for 'tailing' and 'bulging' trout—the latter a term, by the way, new to us in the north—and we desire to give it a further chance before being satisfied ourselves. All we can say about it at present is that we have tried it with varying success, and that we believe it is founded upon natural phenomena.

We do not desire to affect mystery, and would not have mentioned it, only that we have been led up to it, it seems.

VI

FLIES

WE might dismiss this subject much as we have done that of 'Angling Requisites,' but as considerable changes have taken place in Stewart's own disciples' ideas since he recommended his own few standard patterns, we think we must speak at a little greater length of these 'Requisites,' and of certain facts in connection with their use.

The significance of the following opening remarks on the subject of flies, natural and artificial, may perhaps become apparent as we proceed.

Stewart at one place seems almost to refer to the natural insects as reaching the surface of the water from *above*, *i.e.* from the air, whereas, as is well known, the larger number

of species upon which trout fatten reach the
surface from *below, i.e.* hatches out from
the larval stage, on reaching the surface
from the bottom of the stream or channel
bed.

Consequent upon this slip—and we can't
believe it to be other than a *lapsus memoriœ*
—he advocates, as the most deadly moment
of a cast (see *ante*, p. 32), the first alighting
of the artificial fly of the angler. But surely,
if hackle-flies are used, these are sunk, and
while drifting down beneath the surface are
often—nay usually—the more deadly in low,
fine water.

We cannot but believe that Stewart's remarks on page 77, in regard to his estimates
of the innumerable species of insects which
come into life in the summer, are somewhat
exaggerated. This, however, is a question for
an entomologist (and angler) of larger experience and knowledge than there is evidence
of Stewart having been, than we possess,
or possibly even 'Ephemera,' 'Foster,' or
'Pritt.' It seems rather a loose statement.
Did he see this, or only imagine it? Be
that as it may, we think it rather a pity

that he put it forward for the purpose of giving such evidence as follows it. Our experience (be it what it may be deemed worth) is rather opposed to these and to his argument.

Trout show decided preferences for colours (at least educated trout : and trout are becoming better educated—or more frightened —the more any river is fished, flogged, and poled). The actual process is too subtle for our psychological powers, but we think no angler who has studied the subject can fail to realise the changes that have taken place since Stewart wrote.

We find that trout often prefer the new-comer or fresh or later hatched-off insect. Thus a preference for the 'Little Iron Dun' after a gorge of 'Blue Duns' or 'March Browns,' or after 'Greenwell's Glory' has passed over, promptly shows itself. We believe it well to anticipate, say with a red quill or spinner, than to await its actual appearance.

We are of opinion that trout can distinguish colours—though what these colours appear to be to their fishy eyes, through an

aqueous medium, we cannot say, and probably they are very different from our appre-
ciations of the same, looking at them from
our own standpoint, or even up through water
at the sky ' like the fishes.'

It appears to us to be a mere begging of
the question to use as an argument that the
colour of insects, as seen by us, is comparable
with what may be seen by fish. Fish see
through a different medium from ours, and
surely we see differently through theirs. Or
does Stewart mean to uphold that they see
similarly through their medium with us
through ours? We must continue to look
upon colours, to the eye of a fish, as an unknown quality. One fact however is, if
nothing else, suggestive. Many times, when
trying an underhand cast to get the tail-fly
over a rising fish, under an alder or a broken
down reed, has our fly been hung up, and
the tail-fly has been suspended some four
to six inches over his 'wonderful snout,'
and we have seen trout or trouts spring
clear out of water and hook on to that fly,
and, as you may suppose, 'generally stuck
to it too.' This proves they can see through

both media of water and air. The other illustration we like to repeat, viz. the 'man of cubits and the pole,' whose common colour is black! A 'black hackle' is equally a killer on a bright summer day and on a dark moonless night. It is the most killing fly, for instance, on Loch Earn, for both trout and char, when it is too dark for the angler to see his line or flies. This proves they can see as *we can not*. But a white fly—a 'coachman' also kills well on a dark night. Hence arises another phase of the inquiry : Do trout rise best because they see too well, or because they only see movement under differently coloured waters or skies ? Stewart criticises anglers who are too 'scrupulously exact' about a shade of colour (p. 78), but finds fault with their drawing their flies 'up or across the stream.' There is, as we have been trying to show, fault and inconsistency here. But, as an experienced angler friend points out, one inconsistency does not militate against the other group of facts or theories,—we are drifting, however, from facts.

Did Stewart ever see a 'Greenwell's Glory'?

Well, no, of course not: or at least, what he may have seen was not known by that fancy name. [The synonymy of artificial flies is nearly as big a curse as the black gnat.] But, however that may be, Stewart did not include it in his list. And there can be no doubt of its deadly character, either as a floating-bob, or a sunk fly, or with a wing or with only a ragged torn body, not only in Scottish streams but also in Hungary and the Tyrol and in New Zealand.

We do not go with Stewart in his singularly meagre list of standards, good though these undoubtedly are. Stewart in one place seems to consider (p. 81) that a certain colour is more deadly because more readily seen, *i.e.* by the fish, and he instances a black fly as unsurpassed in clear water. We agree with this to some extent, but he says nothing about a 'black hackle' being one of the most deadly flies in a dark night—on Loch Earn, for instance. Or again, what can be said of the grey partridge 'spider' or hackle— light, red, or orange—in clear, low streams in summer, with an equally clear sky? We believe in most circumstances the colours of

the sky above and the water combined gives
a better guide, and that the converse of
Stewart's theory is the true one, viz. that a
'certain colour is more deadly because *less*
readily seen,' and that movement is the
more visible sensation to the eye of a fish.
Thus let us give a few examples :—

We have instanced already 'black hackles'
and 'white coachman' and 'grey spider.' We
have also found a flash of silver tinsel kill
best under a clear blue sky, but also well in
a dark spring water with a clear or sunny
sky.

We have found 'red-body' kill best in a
red water, *i.e.* porter or peat or dark amber.
(Both in salmon-fishing [1] and trout angling.)

But we cannot agree with those who say,

---

[1] Thus a 'Butcher' in a coloured water, a 'Childers'
when the evening sun goes 'back' off a pool. But a
'Jock Scott,' in my experience, has killed as well under
a cloudless sky and low water, or in a dark water, or
under a dark sky. Why? Because we believe the combination of colours which are useful are best harmonised
in the dressing of a 'Jock Scott.' We use 'Wee Jock
Scotties,' and they kill trout well. Dressing : guinea-
fowl hackle, *i.e.* black and white, two small shoulders
of jungle cock (from the top of the bird's head), body
black and yellow, wing pale transparent starling, or
'what you fancy.'

'In a clear water *surely all colours* can be most easily distinguished.' (The italics are ours.) 'Caprice,' spoken of by some, is an utterly undefined quantity and quality. We don't know why trout are called 'capricious.' We believe the 'clerks of the weather,' combined with the 'inspectors of water-works,' have 'cards up their sleeves' about capriciousness! Yet Stewart speaks of 'mere caprice' (p. 81). Surely this is not truly philosophical.

As we have already said, we cannot pin our faith entirely upon Stewart's short list of flies. It may seem an endless matter to discuss, but we would be sorry to have to sally forth to a favourite river-side with no more than Stewart's limited series — good though they undoubtedly are. [Ah! perhaps they may, and did, prove all-sufficient and all-efficient in those palmy days of comparatively unsophisticated trout, just as they might still do all-sufficiently, say, on some far away mountain burn or in some new country.]

We are not going to add more lists of flies to the many confusing names given by scores

of previous writers. We are not sufficiently
able, as accurate 'entomologists,' to distinguish all the innumerable shades, dressings,
and fancy names applied to the earlier and
later hatches-off of the four 'up-winged' flies
of Foster. Nor can we attempt to reconcile
all those fancy flies with their natural con-
geners. We were never good at nomenclature
even in its purely zoological aspects, and we
would be content to follow the lead of ' the
latest authority' in such matters. But who
is? Is it Foster, Theakstone, or Pritt? Even
in their own country they don't appear
to use the same nomenclature. It would
prove a serviceable piece of work if some
entomologist and experienced angler would
take this question of nomenclature in hand
and settle it, and reconcile all the different
local names under the true insects' names.
None of the many angling books which we
have seen and possess do so in a simple,
easily-referred-to way. Foster's, we think,
is the best, and next Theakstone and Pritt,
but they don't agree in their nomenclature.
Then, besides authors, there are other con-
fusions, worse confounded, introduced by fly-

dressers, and named perhaps after some
gentleman angler, who has had it 'launched
off' in the *Field* or elsewhere, such as the
'Francis fly,' and scores of others. We
cannot do without our salmon flies so
named, because we cannot call them aught
else than 'Jock Scott,' 'Childers,' 'Black and
Blue Doctor,' etc. etc., but it seems a very
different occasion to introduce fancy names
for trout flies, where it is possible to allocate
them to their natural relatives. Some no
doubt there are which often do noble service,
and as it is not pretended that they imitate
any natural insect—or at least any known
insect—such must be retained. The pro-
bability is, however, that they do imitate
some insect accidentally, or otherwise that
their colours are blended in such a way as to
command success under certain conditions of
light and *colour*, and of *water* and *sky*. We
believe the whole question may yet be found
to resolve itself into what we have before
referred to, a consideration of light and
colour effects. How otherwise is it that on
some days trout allow flotillas of 'March
Browns' and flotillas of 'Early Duns' to float

past utterly unheeded, as often they are known to do, and as we have often seen them do ? At other times they rise and miss the flies time after time. Some one (is it Theakstone ?) says the 'Yellow Sally' is 'bitter, and trout don't like them.' We never eat any ourselves. Certain it is 'Yellow Sally' or its imitations not very often proves acceptable, but there are few rules without the exceptions that prove them; and we have filled a basket almost entirely with 'Yellow Sally,' *once* on the Ythan, and once also with the 'Grannom'[1] on the same stream— or at least with the fly nearest to it which we had in our book when it came on,—at other times with 'Yellow Sally' on the stream not a trout moved at them, but the 'little iron dun' killed. The trout were not touching the natural floating 'Yellow Sally.' In this connection we desire to call attention to a small array of facts placed here in tabular arrangement,[2] by which we try to compare the colours of the spectrum or rainbow colours, the fixed colours of Hay,

---

[1] We never saw the Grannom on Ythan before or since that occasion. [2] *V.* p. 53.

D

and the flies, both salmon and trout, which
we would employ under such colours or
approximate colours of water and sky.

When the water is just clearing from
'yellow' or 'clay' or 'pea-soup' (see scale
and gauge, p. 169) to 'drumly,' and before
or during the 'porter' or 'peat' stage, and
when it is too high to fish comfortably up,
or to wade against, and standing well back
from the lip and casting across is the order
of the day, then a large red hackle, a 'wood-
cock-and-red,' a 'teal-and-red,' or a fly with
some red in it ought to be on the cast.

When the water is in the above condition,
with varying skies and big white clouds,
very often trout are found to rise short; but
when the water clears a little more, say to
light porter or dark amber, then trout often
take very surely and very keenly, if the flies
above mentioned are large enough, and trout
will even begin to rise at smaller flies if
amongst froth or in an eddy.

When the 'light amber' stage is reached,
we believe in yellow flies, but some degree of
further selection may always be caused by
the colour of the sky and reflections. A 'pro-

fessor,' a 'grouse and yellow,' or an 'early
dun,' or a 'March brown' with light wing and
yellow twist (or the female), or a large 'Greenwell's glory' with gold-rib. Or if the river is
lower and sizes have to be reduced, then the
medium sizes of Walbran's hackles—'waterhen and gold-rib,' 'waterhen bloa,' 'watchet'
'small iron dun,' 'snipe bloa,' etc. 'Early
duns' ought to be dressed very light and with
three shades at least of wing (woodcock,
starling, and corn bunting). A 'red-spinner'
kills best in medium water in the 'amber'
stage or higher, even to 'drumly' if big
enough.

When 'clear' and 'crystal' are reached
the hackles begin to come in: black, grey,
partridge and orange, partridge and yellow,
grey partridge, priest (see list, etc.), and Walbran's hackles. Black hackles, with slight
purply gloss in the larger sizes, but plain, dull
black in the smaller sizes, are always useful,
but perhaps most so in the lower stages of
water. A 'Zulu,' *i.e.* black hackle with red tag,
is more useful in darker water. A 'partridge'
and blue body is sometimes useful as a midsummer fly under a blue sky, and a 'grey .

partridge' under a cloudy sky. A 'partridge'
and green body we have never done much
with, but we can believe it would kill at
certain times where water was much over-
hung by vivid green foliage, or when that
peculiar green reflection is observed—usually
towards evening of a summer day. 'Alders'
and 'sedges' are useful, especially towards
evening—indeed, the 'alder' is a general
favourite at the right time, and will often
kill well into the summer.

At one time, not so very long ago, the
popular belief was in a *dark* fly for a bright
day or clear water, and a *light* fly for dark
water or dark sky. Now, we believe, anglers
of experience and with sufficient scientific
interest in their practice, believe in the converse states of combinations, viz. a dark fly
in a dark water and sky, and a light fly in
a bright water and sky.

In the Table we make an attempt to
relegate certain flies—salmon and trout—
for general selection in differently coloured
waters and under differently coloured skies
and clouds and weathers. There may prove
to be enough suggestion in it to induce

Salmon Flies	Trout Flies	Colours—Water.	Colours—Sky.	Hay's Colours.	Rainbow Colours.
1. Lady Caroline Butcher Childers Popham Jock Scott	Red Spinner Red Hackle Teal and Red Wickham Pheasant, etc.	Porter, Peat	Dark, Lurid, or Roving	Red	Red
2. Jock Scott Canary Lady Grace, and smaller sizes	Professor Woodcock and Yellow Partridge and Orange Duns	Amber	Cloudy or Roving	Orange	Orange
3. Large sizes—same	Large sizes, same	Yellow	Usually bad skies	Yellow	Yellow
4. Green Highlander Blue Doctor	Part. and Green	Green or Bluish, such as Derbyshire wye	Green tree reflections Blue sky	Green	Green
5. Blue Doctor Blue Jock Scott Silver Doctor Dusty Miller	Black Hackle Black and Silver Wee Jock Scottie Snipe and Purple, and Hackles	Blue, Cloudless	Clear or Crystal	Blue	Blue
6. See 1.	Red flies, as above, 1.	Brown, clearing	Blue, cloudless, or dark	Purple or Black	Indigo
7. Black Doctor Jock Scott Silver Doctor Dusty Miller Spey flies, with long, filmy hackles	Priest Saltoun Black Hackle Duns Walbran's Hackles Grey Partridge Part. and Blue Part. and Red Part. and Yellow Wee Jock Scottie	Clear, Crystal Amber ,,	High cirrus Grey, White Blue ,,		Violet to Grey-White

others to take up the idea and work it out more completely. As it at present stands it is confessedly imperfect. But we are inclined to believe there is sufficient material even here for fairly safe deductions.

Possibly (but this is theoretical) proof may yet be forthcoming that the reason why *some* flies—natural flies, I mean—are not such favourites with the fish, lies in the colour of the flies, and their greater or less visibility under certain colours of water and sky and sun and reflections, and not necessarily *upon their flavour*. We think the study is still obscure, but one worthy of some further considering by anglers and entomologists.

The following are some notes kept upon the appearances of the natural insects on the water :

1893. April 27th, Stonefly out.[1]
   ,,   ,,   28th, Some rusty blue duns.
   ,,   May   3rd, Little iron blue.
1894. April 16th, Stray rise of March browns.
   ,,   ,,   18th, A few blue duns.

---

[1] *We* speak of Stonefly as the perfect insect of the creeper.

1894. April 19th, A small rise of olive duns;
                      Stonefly out.

,,   ,,   28th, (Forglen) Jenny-spinners out.

,,   May 11th, Great rise of Grannom.

,,   ,,   19th, (Snow and hail) Iron blue out.

1895. April 17th, Small rise of March browns
                      and a few blue duns.

,,   ,,   20th, No fly at Rothiemay, but a
                      heavy rise of March browns
                      on Avochie. Condition of
                      trout rapidly improving.

,,   ,,   21st, Large rise of Grannoms.

,,   ,,   22nd, Stonefly out.

,,   ,,   25th, Sprinkling of olive duns.

,,   ,,   27th, One trout chokeful of Stonefly
                      and creepers; a good deal of
                      olive duns.

,,   ,,   28th, Large rise of iron blues.

1896. April 16th, Small mobs of blue duns at
                      intervals; no March browns.

,,   ,,   24th, A few blue duns which are
                      taking; March browns ap-
                      pear about over.

,,   ,,   27th, A very few small duns.

,,   ,,   28th, A good many yellow-legged
                      duns.

,,   ,,   30th, Large rise of blue duns.

,,   May   7th, Grannom out, but trout did
                      not seem to care for them.

,,   ,,   15th, A few little iron blues.

The above are taken from Mr. C. H.

Alston's Registers, kept at Rothiemay and Avochie.

The following were kept in our own Registers at Laithers in the season of 1898 :

1898. April 11th, Creepers and stoneflies (trout are in fair condition). Small hatches of March browns, about 11 A.M.

„   „   22nd, Early blue duns, 10.50 to 1 P.M.

1898. April 30th, till ⎫ Iron blues off and on, but
       May 30th,   ⎭   not in quantity.

„   April 27th, Yellow Sally and olive dun up but very few, and trout not rising. Iron blue came on and we killed four with it.

Small black gnats constant on the water and in froth all May more or less.

Trout long since had deteriorated in condition (see tables of measurements and weights) and going back in colour—this is certain, on this reach of water this year.

1898. April 30th, Yellow Sally came on at 12
and continued till 1, and
again at 3 P.M., but trout
not rising to them. Iron
blues came on then also, but
trout not moving.

VII

ON TROUTING WITH THE FLY—THE PRACTICE

I⊤ has been often said to us: 'In rough water of a small stream, with dead low summer level—no use.' We say, 'Give to me.'

Stalk that stream, creep and crawl, if necessary, up towards its tail-race or glide. Then cast rapidly *once only* over each likely spot you can easily reach with a line, say, *not more* than twice the length of your rod, less if possible, letting your flies—two in number —rest each cast one or two seconds, and keeping the line itself as much out of the water as possible. This done, then remember you have only attracted the attention of the *best* fish in the swim.

Now once more come over the same water,

beginning straight up on your own side,
then farther out and more across, then
farther, until among the last casts from
the same standpoint you are fishing straight
across, having gradually slightly lengthened
line. After each cast allow your flies to
come down towards your feet, or abreast of
you. Never use a longer line than you can
keep taut from rod-tip to tail-fly, except
possibly the last few casts across, if you wish
to reach over. When a fish rises, 'turn the
key' gently, pull down-stream, *kill all you
hook*, land them below your standpoint, so
as not to disturb unfished water above ;
then take one or two steps up, still kneel-
ing or creeping, and repeat the process. If
you are on the left bank of the stream, cast
over the right shoulder when you begin to
fish up and across, and each cast recover
in the same direction; thus you cover the
water with the two flies. Supposing it a
small stickle of very shallow water, raise
the hand towards the right, and the flies
come down opposite one another. If you
did the contrary the flies would come down
with the current one on the top of the other

or along the same line. This cannot be avoided if you are fishing the first cast or so straight up stream. The pace at which considerable reaches of water can be accurately covered thus by two or three flies, according to the size of the river, depends upon the amount of knowledge and experience of the best lies of the fish, and in the activity, endurance, youth, and prompt manipulation of the angler. It should be remembered that to cover the largest number of rising fish and pick out the *best* ones, thoroughly and scientifically, especially when they are taking free, the casting and getting over the water should be as rapid as possible. The above remarks apply particularly to the lower stages of the water, say 0. 0. 0. 0^2. of scale (*q.v.* p. 169), but the same method may be employed, and the same care taken, when the river is in a more flushed condition, up to, say, 0 0 (medium) and amber colour, though in these higher conditions it may not be so *necessary* for success. As to the time of year, that is immaterial in such practice, but always if the river is low and clear or crystal. We

repeat, striking from the reel in such fishing is a mere waste of muscular energy.
Lightness of hand, keenness of eye, steady
application, are seemlier, quieter, quicker.
The muscular arm effect, judging from the
excited contortions some anglers indulge in
who 'strike from the reel,' is a sheer need-
less waste of vital force.   Let me repeat,
the true action is as you would 'Turn a
key in a well-oiled lock, quickly and quietly
but firmly, with a scarcely perceptible, yet
decided, raising from the wrist.'

But, if you are fishing up either with or
against a strong breeze, too strong for comfortable fishing, as is often experienced, and
when it is often extremely difficult to prevent
your line from 'bellying' *in* the water, and *by*
the wind, even when short, *then* often vigorous
striking is necessary in order to convey the
action quick enough to the terminal strands.
At all other times 'quiet and gentle but
firm' does it.   The angler who can fish a
reach or succession of streams and pools
and broken water, quickly and quietly as
above, has ten times more pleasure than the
' man of cubits and a pole.'   He kills better

fish and more of them; he fishes over perhaps one-fourth or one-fifth of the extent of
river which the down-stream fisher does,
and lays his *flies* (not his *line*, necessarily)
over every feeding fish that is reachable; he
disturbs the water scarcely at all; and he
frightens and renders shy not one-tenth of
the fish which the man does who 'throws
the long shadows o'er the pool.'

If you find a good trout 'rising short' (of
which we will have more to say) or refusing
on a second or even third application, remember that that may be caused by some
tiny swirl or eddy, though it may also arise
from other different causes. Therefore it may
be worth while, in the case of a good trout,
to alter your standpoint and try again (see
ante, p. 36, and *infra*, p. 64). The great
pull an up-stream angler possesses over the
'down-streamer' is well expressed by Stewart
in the last two sentences on p. 110.[1] The
hurried dash made at a fly crossing the
stream in jerks and jumps, almost certainly
often account for what is termed 'short-
rising.' But that 'short-rising' occurs from
this alone we do not credit, and later on, we

[1] Refer to Stewart's book.

hope to point out what appears to us to be undoubted causes, noted from many comparative averages and innumerable notes (see under chapter on ' Worm-fishing,' and discussion of ' weathers,' chap. viii.).

If a river rises or maintains a higher level than medium, or if it be slightly coloured, say, reddish or darker than amber, and just rather deep for comfortable wading, then good fishing may be had by standing well back from the river verge, or well back from the lip of a steep bank, and casting opposite your feet, with three flies, and let them float down (or drift down) close under your own side, casting rapidly, and rarely allowing your flies to get below your standpoint.

Stewart advises the angler ' always to keep on the shallow side of a stream, because the best trout generally lie under the bank on the deep side.' This has not been our invariable experience. Sometimes—often, we may say—we have with advantage waded, where wading was practicable on the deeper side, when fish were feeding on the shallows, and cast out and over on to the shallows. Additional concealment is often thus afforded, and, according to our experience, the best fish are

not necessarily on the deep side, nor under
the bank, when on the feed.

The smooth glides above streams or pools
are often superior spots holding the 'monarch'
of the pool, especially where the stream,
before the rush, contracts. A 'monarch'
there holds the 'key of the pantry,' as it were,
and may often be taken when there is barely a
ruffle or a break on the surface, and especially
if there be a light amber tint in the water.

Many an angler appears to us to waste half
his time in vain repetitions, as if he could
force the trout to take, and as if he could not
satisfy himself in two or three casts at most
as to whether he was doing it properly. An
angler new to a stream certainly stands at
some disadvantage to the local man, all else
being equal, who knows every rock and
stone, turn and twist of the water. And as
we have already pointed out, there are
occasions—plenty of them, too—where such
a policy as continuous and rapid casting, and
shifting one's standpoint, is often valuable.
But it should not be practised except where
the angler's experience tells him it may be
remunerative—such as if a swirl or back
eddy is known (or seen) to hold a good fish.

An advocate of down-stream fishing once stated in our hearing, if not indeed in black and white, ' If it were not that the up-stream angler selected his spots, he would have no chance with the down-streamer.' To this we reply, ' We prefer trout-angling to salmon-fishing for trout,' and the beauty of fishing up appears to us to be the knowledge acquired and the natural *selection* which follows such education.

Many, indeed most, anglers prefer to fish down, when heavy down-stream winds render it too difficult and too fatiguing to fish up; and, indeed, in such weather there are many days in which the up-stream casts are made almost impossible. But Stewart advocates the attempt even then. It is possible at times to fight the wind across by a peculiar underhand flick, difficult to describe and not always easy to attain to, sending out the line on the same plane with the surface of the water; but this requires a stiff rod, and cannot be said to be very satisfactory. Another plan is to cover a larger mileage of water, and thereon select only such bends or reaches as are negotiable. We have taken many a fair

E

basket in this way under adverse circumstances. A third way—and where neither of the above are found to be practicable—is to take Stewart's advice as conveyed on pp. 117-118, and 'you will be more able to fish properly' another time.

An angler friend of experience writes:— 'Yes; I have no doubt whatever, from experience, that the underhand cast is the best plan for getting one's line out against, or rather "under," the wind.' We have said it is difficult to describe, as well as not always easy to do, but perhaps the following may convey the idea:—The action is somewhat similar to that of a round-hand bowler, when, at the end of his swing, and keeping his hand low—rather below the shoulder than above—he attempts to put a 'break back' upon the ball at the pitch. And in angling, and attempting to dodge a flaw of wind, the same motion, as when he tries to 'put on a twist' from leg in cricket. But in angling the whole action is not an entire arm-action, but should be done by forearm and wrist only.

VIII

THE CAPTURE

Now, as regards capturing your fish, and landing or netting them, I have some words to say, which may not be looked upon as safe guides. Indeed, I scarcely feel inclined to preach to others what in this respect I practise (I speak here in the first person singular, for I believe I am almost singular about it). [1]

First, let me say :—I have never taken kindly to a landing-net, nor a landing-net to me. I have possessed many—one after another—and I have always looked upon them as an unnecessary incumbrance and impediment to rapid up-stream fishing. I know I may fail (but neither do I expect)

[1] We believe a well-known angler of Perth accounts for many of his large baskets by utilising a somewhat similar method.

to convince others. But I will say what I
practise. I hold that any trout above half
a pound is worth going to shore with, but
that nine-tenths of fairly well-hooked half-
pounders can be creeled by hand, but not
necessarily as Stewart advises; indeed, my
plan is the *very one* he strongly condemns.

Stewart says:—' In taking the trout out of
the water do so with your hands, if you have
not a landing-net, and never attempt lifting it
by the line, or you are almost certain to pay
dearly for your experience.' To this I would
add the rider: 'Unless you do so the correct
way.' All I can say is—though I confess to
losing many good trout, as every angler of
experience has also done—my method and
results show *much time* saved, *temper* saved
from entanglements or 'fankles' with a net,
or in *wading* out to the bank, and a high
average, *in my own case*, of successful basket-
ing of trout *up to* and, *when well hooked*,
over the half-pound. If trout be very lightly
hooked, the risk of the plan is of course increased, but this fact can usually be ascertained before *taking the trout by hands*,
and if so, then the shore may be sought,

or the net used. Even when I carry a net, I prefer my method for all trout under or up to the half-pound. And now, having advocated my method, I will endeavour to describe it.

This method is *almost* what Stewart utterly condemns (*v.* p. 111). But I hold there is a correct and very safe way of landing trout besides that of taking them in the water by the hand or hands. There is a fairly safe way of doing it, and an absolutely dangerous way of doing it. I will first describe my plan, and then give instances of its success. I may add that a fishing companion unwilling to be convinced has often watched me do it and confessed it was 'good.' I will try and describe what I almost invariably do when wading out from shore with a twelve-foot split-cane rod by Hardy, with a half-pound or often a three-quarter-pound trout on:—Play out the fish until you can keep his head and mouth out of water, *keeping steady strain* as you would do if bringing him to net. Preserving the same strain, no more and no less, and having wound up line till you can raise the top back over your shoulder,

gently lift by the last gut strand as near to
the fish's head as you can with the right
hand, dropping at the same time the point of
the rod, and a second after drop the rod itself
into the hollow of the right arm. Lift the
fish by the same steady, never increasing
nor diminishing strain, and carefully avoid-
ing any jerking, until it hangs limp and
played out, opposite say the third or fourth
button of your coat or waistcoat. Seize the
fish with the left hand simultaneously with
its touching your breast. Thus you have
both hands free to disengage the hook.
But, before doing that, break his neck against
the under side of your right-hand wrist.
('Blood!' says some one, but that is easily
guarded against by a protecting cuff and a
pad, or if you are fishing in a waterproof it
will wash!) Then, retaining the same hold
of the fish, release the hook, and basket your
fish in your pannier, which, I presume, you
carry on the left side, or under the left arm,
with a Foster-strap. *Voila!*

Now, we have often in a day's fishing
quietly lifted *every* fish under and up to the
half-pound when wading; and out of a basket

of, say, thirteen to fifteen or twenty pounds, with the average at the half-pound (in the river Deveron) lost only one or two trout. This, of course, includes larger trout, say three-quarter-pound to one and a quarter or larger, which I took to bank, or netted if I was 'possessed *by* a landing-net.' This proportion, I flatter myself, will compare well with any work in which all were taken to shore or entangled in a net.[1]

I do not ask my readers to accept this method, but I back myself to do it all through a season with much advantage. Of course there are occasions on which a net is almost absolutely indispensable, and these occasions do not require recapitulation, just as there are plenty occasions when a half-pound trout and even larger can be gently lifted (not jerked or 'bunged' out) bodily from the top-rod strain, and safely deposited at your feet—not swung over head as if trying to emulate Mark Twain's ant going over Strasburg steeple. What in salmon-fishing

---

[1] Somewhat similar advice, however, is given by the author of the *Angler and the Loop Rod*, p. 107, though recorded somewhat differently and the method not just the same.

is also known as 'hand-lining a kelt,' applies equally to the method I speak of, only that in the case of a trout of the dimensions 'I speak of, it is actually *lifted*, not by the *line*, but by the terminal *strand of gut*.

IX

WORM IN CLEAR WATER

'Those who despise worm-fishing as a thing so
simple as to be quite unworthy of their attention, would quickly discover their mistake if
brought to a small, clear water on a warm day
in June or July.'—(Stewart, p. 135.)

But thundery weather, dark sky, heavy
cumuli-clouds piling up round the horizon
with little or no motion, or in different cur-
rents, or desperate down-stream gales in
June, and worse still, in July, are usually
fatal to anglers' success—though even on such
days, here and there, some fish may be got.

Stewart advocates a 'double-handed rod on
all occasions, in all waters, whether small or
large.' All we can say is, we do *not* consider
such necessary, and it is certainly not so
pleasant and sporting to fish with.

If a long rod is at any time required or
advisable, it is upon the *smaller* streams,

where one cannot comfortably wade, or on boisterous days when it is almost too fatiguing to try. In larger streams, even where very shallow, and the shadow of your rod can be kept off the water you are fishing, a shorter and stiff rod is all that is required, if the angler wades. We use generally a twelve-foot split-cane Hardy. We find it ample with a line from half as long again as the rod, to at most twice the length—the latter only used occasionally.

Of other worm-anglers' requisites we need not speak, as anglers can best please themselves with two-hook, three-hook, or four-hook tackles, or fine single wires, all of which have their own advocates.

'The best rate for the worm to travel at is undoubtedly the natural one, and if the trout wish to seize it they have plenty of time to do so' (p. 142).

Their education is up to that standard! Therefore we rarely use sinkers, except under certain circumstances. Instance, in high water, when one would be better employed in *howkin' worms*. Or in a heavy down-stream wind, when, after all, one would be

better not practising 'Quixotic exercises.'
In a heavy down-stream wind it is not a
pleasing or edifying exercise 'throwing back
expletives at the rough-tongued winds!' any
more than it is satisfactory to 'kick against
the pricks.' In such weather it is better
to search out the few bends and reaches
where the wind blows locally up, as in fly-
fishing. Under these conditions we grant,
if one is determined to fish, a thirteen-foot
stiff rod and a heavier line is an advantage;
but it becomes a regular 'poling' match, unless
it can be wielded by one hand comfortably.
We have *not* experience of steel-centred rods
and lines. Of course, if an angler has only
an odd holiday to devote to fishing, then he
is right to 'pole.'

In a heavy down-stream wind the worm
travels at 'railway speed,' owing to the combined influence of wind-drag and water-drag.
Such is inevitable; and, as in *good up-stream
worming* as little of the line as possible
should be *in the water*, even under the
best conditions, any one may conceive how
impossible it must be to preserve the same,
when all the conditions are adverse. *Lower*

'the top after the cast until all your line is
submerged,' says some one.   No use, sir; the
water-drag is how many times greater!
And how many times faster is the travel
of the bait! 'Put on sinkers and fish with
a stiffer rod,' says another advocate.   Very
well, perhaps that is the best way; but even
then, does the worm travel naturally? the
sinker may act as a drag if attached a foot
or two up the line, and *more* or *less* assist,
and such fishing is, we know, often successful.   And if people will fish, or must fish
when they have only a short time to select
their days, and if they will preserve their
equanimity, and not 'speak back,' and are
supplied with plenty of sinkers mounted on
rotten gut for attachments (*when others are
lost*), and still enjoy themselves, and can
get their line straight to where they want
to place it, this plan is no doubt the best.

But another potent reason we believe is:—
That the best-fed and larger class of trout
are not feeding on the shallows when a gale
of wind is tearing down-stream.   (By better
class of fish we mean up to the average of
the stream.)   This is all the more the case, if,

as has usually been their practice, the better trout have been feeding during the night. Stewart says:—'Streams in the immediate neighbourhood of large pools will generally be found the best, as the trout come from the pools into the streams to feed.' But when the conditions we describe supervene—and in summer the wind usually rises as the day advances—these best trout, which have been on the feed at night, fall back into the pools if they find a 'rough-tongued' breeze and unfavourable conditions. Large, well-fed fish leave the shallows at such times to the small fry, and probably sleep (?); and the par and juveniles, being young and active, then have a high old time, and 'eat the gooseberries in the garden,' so to speak.

Every angler knows how particularly annoying par and small trout are on some days more than on others. If a large trout is on the prowl, or has taken up his special feeding-lie in a stream, he commands the 'key of the situation,' and is not slow to repel all minor fry that come within many feet of his 'monarchical throne.' This we have often seen when looking down into

the clear water from a height. Even before
taking the bait himself, he will chase away
the small fry, *i.e.* if the bait is lying stationary
at his very nose. If it be travelling, his dash
at it is enough in itself to scare the smaller
fish. Therefore—at least we feel *sure* it is
one good reason—the small fry feed when
he is not there.

But with adverse winds, *still* a basket may
be made if the angler *covers more mileage of
river, and selects only such bends or reaches
which are partially or wholly negotiable,*
just as may be done in fly-fishing; and we
have seen good baskets made in this way.
Still, it is not invariably the case that big
fish are not on the feed during a strong
down-stream wind. If they are found on
the shallows and streams in such circumstances, we certainly think other countervailing reasons are discoverable in each case.
In the worm season, as we have said, the
wind *usually* increases as day advances. As
for trout feeding under *all* circumstances of
heavy down-winds, *that* we cannot believe;
but that they do so at times is certain, as
may be gathered from the following quota-

tion from a letter from an expert up-stream fisher :—' My own experience is to put on a lead shot and fish up-stream (with a long rod?). . . . I remember well a typical day with nearly a gale blowing down. Even with the aid of a sinker I could not even get a rod's length of line out, and often it went splash into the water in a most unfisherman-like way. Yet, spite of these disadvantages, I never had such a good take, and never had so many extra large trout. A hard down-stream wind helps one little in quick streams ; but near the tops and at the tails of pools, where big ones are fond of lying, and where it is impossible to fish them in fine water— the only legitimate worm-water in ordinary conditions—the strong wind gives sufficiently rough water to hide the fisher, though using only a very short line. As regards the pleasure, however,' he adds, ' of fishing under these conditions, that is a matter of taste. I must confess, after the day's fishing re-ferred to, I felt mentally and physically (fizzi-cally? P.D.) done, with wading up-stream and exerting all my strength casting, though I had a good basket of magnificent fish. I must

confess that my mind was a jumble of wind
and water, fish and worms, and a line doing
its best to knot round the rod, the fisher, or
anything it could get hold of; in fact, do
anything but keep in the water.'

We think the above is a very accurate
description of what most people may feel
after such a day's experience, even with a
fair basket of trout and a bellyful of whisky.

Personally, we prefer to cover more river-
bank and look for the nooks and corners
where the wind is not so frisky.

The following is from the *Fishing Gazette*
of a date I have unfortunately lost:—

'There is yet another way of dealing with a
head wind, which Mr. Tod may possibly not
have heard of. It was one of the lessons of my
mentor, the late Dickie Routledge, of Carlisle.
I had been telling him a distressing experience
with the wind in my teeth, and had asked him
what he would do under such circumstances.
'Fish down-stream,' said he, and showed me how
he did it. He made his cast (right hand of
course) with the left shoulder and foot advanced,
and when the bait dropped, swung his body
steadily round and took one step forward with
the right foot. The bait thus travelled about

two yards. By that time he had either hooked a trout or demonstrated that there was not one to get hold of. I never practically tested this method, for the simple reason that one would have to go to the top of the water, instead of beginning at the bottom and fishing-up as one naturally does in practising the clear water worm, so I always preferred to fish up and chance it.

GRETA.'

We never tried Routledge's plan; but he was (*is*, we hope) a good fisherman, well known on his native streams and, journeying occasionally to 'Scottish waters,' and we can well credit the plan. It is, it seems to us, something like fishing across with fly, when standing back from the bank in a high water, as we have tried to describe above under 'Fly-fishing Practice.' The difference is, presumably, that Routledge wades in fine water when he does it, whereas, in fly-fishing so, it is usually when one *cannot wade*, and in higher water, and concealment is not necessary—or *less* necessary. We cannot feel sure, however, that demonstration could simply show 'that the trout was not there,' because, far oftener than not, such a cast is drawn blank even when the wind is *up*. Few trout are killed *below* the angler's standpoint—*i.e.* lower down — even under the most favourable conditions of wind and water.[1] *Perhaps*— we do not know—the *down-stream heavy* wind may, in such a case, make *that* form of cast, or 'point,' *more* favourable.   But *why*, we cannot at the time conceive, though we may find out if we practise it, which we intend to do.

[Thanks to Greta for the tip, and though unknown to me by *nom-de-plume*, by leave we wish to send him 'greetings' in all good fellowship.]

Sometimes it is useful to the angler to know when it is wise to change from fly to worm, or *vice versa*, especially about the commencement of the worm season.   A simple way, and quite a good way, is to bite off your tail-fly and terminal strand of gut, and affix your worm-tackle in its place. We have often caught trout thus upon both fly and worm—sometimes at the same cast. In no ways do we find the action of the one interfered with by that of the other—rather indeed an *aid*, if you keep the bob-fly on the

---

[1] *i.e.* in worming in *fine water*.

surface. It makes a good guide to the eye
if your line stops.

We made a fine basket on the Whitadder
on a cool, drizzly day, with east wind, in
July, with blinks of sun now and then, by
this combination of fly and worm, and this
was the first time we had at that period ever
fished that river. The reach was that between
Abbey St. Bathans nearly to Ellemford, and
we fished it after two other anglers who had
fished in the early morning had taken down
their rods and left. We began about 10.45,
having driven over from Grant's House, and
continued fishing with varying success up to
about four, when the trout stopped apparently
for good. We had forty-eight trout—just
twelve pounds; and as we at that time had
never fished a well-whipped Border stream,
we felt fairly elated; and a local angler
from Duns, whom we met there—Roger by
name—said, 'Man, ye've gotten a grand
tak';' and afterwards, 'Ay, I mind ye.
Man, ye had a *graund* basket thon day last
year.' Roger at that time fished as a pro-
fessional angler for the White Swan Hotel,
Duns, and he and I passed several days

together afterwards by the river-side from
Ellemford upwards. We have rather spun
out our tale in trying to show how useful
this combination may sometimes be. We
got quite one-half of our basket with fly,
whilst the worm was attached at the tail;
but the *best* trout were taken by the worm.

In the worm season, if a trout be seen to
rise at a fly, it is almost certain that that
trout will take the worm if it is carefully
and correctly presented.

The extent to which water is oxygenated
by air is an undoubted factor, we consider,
in the happy and active existence of *Salmo
fario.* 'The livelier the water the livelier
the fish,' as a general rule, though we don't
mean to say there may not be some exceptions arising out of countervailing circumstances.

Of large and small worms, of 'green' or
well-scoured worms we can say nothing new.
Yet we have met with anglers—clear-water
anglers, too, of good practice—who have
upheld 'green' worms against small red
ones, 'because the former have more smell.'
'The beetle-crawler' has some right to defend

the green worm, but *sight* surely is the sense utilised more than *smell* in low, clear water. Besides, fishes' sense of smell seems to us still to remain an 'unknown quantity,' and as yet *unproved*.

It is unnecessary to recapitulate the *advantages* of up-stream fishing with worm. Nothing can be added to that part of the subject beyond Stewart's directions for practice. But when we come to speak of when to expect sport, while his directions and facts are in most cases incontrovertible, we think there has been left some room for deductions as to the 'whys' and 'wherefores' of good and bad conditions, and we propose in the next chapter to explain some of these matters of inquiry.

WEATHERS AND ELECTRICAL DISTURBANCES

STEWART's definitions of weathers is a most valuable part of his treatise. If we take his 'worst of all'—that combination, 'bright sky and sun, with a few clouds and strong west wind' (or, we would add, down-stream wind), causing a glare or glitter on the water, making it *too difficult for the fish to see* the rapidly travelling bait (or fly), we can readily see the reason why, as he adds in a rider—'On such a day, early morning is the best time.'

But this fact and conclusion point to another phase or phenomenon in connection with the 'time of the take,' which is perhaps more applicable under fly-fishing than worm-fishing, and has also to do with the 'short rising' of both trout and salmon at fly. As we believe it has to do with worm-fishing, though perhaps in a less degree, we think perhaps this is as good a place as any to speak of it in detail.

The 'times of the take' vary in different rivers. But we have often thought that after fishing a reach *up* when the sun was on the shoulder, or even behind the angler, up to twelve or one o'clock in the day, especially in April and May, and having had fair success at the 'time of the take,' which usually runs from eight A.M. to twelve or one o'clock, and then fishing again the same or a similarly disposed reach of water with poor success after the sun had so far passed the meridian, and was blazing downstream in the eyes of the fish as well as in those of the angler,—we have thought that Stewart's combination of bad weathers and sky were accounted for by the difficulty the fish had in *seeing* the lures, whether worm or fly; in fact, that sun and certain lights and colour-effects often effectually put down well-fed and large trout, but that small trout or par or large ill-fed trout still try to feed. Often when they do, it happens that the floating-fly or even the sunk-hackle is *missed*? Temperatures of air and water have also to do with the rising or non-rising of fish. The 'time of the take,' which is often, if not always, equivalent with the time of the hatch-off of insects in sufficient quantity, may also, and doubtless *is*, in measure dependent upon the action of the sun at certain angles to the plane of the water or to the bed of the stream.

As for 'short rising,' who among trout- and salmon-fishers is not acquainted with the phenomena which often occur, viz.:—certain conditions of water and sky, amongst which are Stewart's 'bad weathers'—such as, in heavy waters, in coloured waters, in heavy down-stream winds, in electric and glittery skies, in leaden-hued water, on calm, sultry days? Never—well, almost never—have we seen good baskets made on such days, unless a change intervenes; nor on days when criss-cross winds and flaws of 'rough-tongued,' un-steady winds 'waff' the water in all directions. How often have anglers, including ourselves, sat by the river-side watching the 'herring fleet of "early duns" or "March browns"

sailing down the stream,' and seen the great
'splutter' of trout making frantic saltations—
'playing,' some call it (poor play for them)!
How often do we fix our eye upon a single
'March brown' until he passes into the swirl
where a big trout lies, eager to feed, and see
him *missed*, and then see that same trout
miss five or six others in succession! Play!
How often do we watch the same fly missed
by three, four, or more trout in succession!
Are they all playing? No; *but* they *are*
'*rising short.*'

We do not uphold that the 'short rising'
of salmon can be explained in an absolutely
similar way to that of trout, but we feel
very sure there are close affinities between
the two sets of phenomena. We have, however, always kept notes in our Salmon
Registers of the time of day when we have
killed or risen, pricked, lightly hooked, and
lost salmon and grilse, and such can hardly
fail to prove educative; but as we are really
writing of trout-fishing we pass on here,
though we may refer to this again.

Now, if to the above natural adverse circumstances be added the unnatural jerking of

larval imitations, or full-winged flies across
and up a stream,—while these motions may
slightly neutralise the action, and trout be
thereby induced to rise, still, what is the
usual result? Possibly a basket of small
trout, but far more pricked and lost, and a
large proportion foul-hooked. We have seen
nearly fifty per cent. of a basket of trout which
were foul-hooked, even by an up-stream
angler, and usually under the conditions we
have tried to describe. One day in 1898
we got thirteen trout (eight pounds) during
a short spell of trout-rising, of which six
were foul-hooked and many others pricked,
light-hooked, and lost. (For further details
consult the several Tables given further on
showing actual days of fishing described.)
The above is only one of many similar experiences.

An instance has been given where artificial
electric light had prompt effect in putting
down rising fish. This is related in an
admirable little treatise by Mr. Spachman
on New Zealand trout.[1] A searchlight was

[1] *Trout in New Zealand*, published by authority at
Wellington, New Zealand, 1882, p. 27 *q.v.*

thrown upon clouds at an angle (correct?) of forty-five degrees. This cast a reflection upon a river twelve miles off. The river was the Opihí. Trout had been rising freely to an angler's lures up to the time (to the moment) the glare came upon the water, and then they suddenly ceased. Similar effects had been observed under similar circumstances on other rivers of New Zealand. From this it may appear that the effect upon trout may be less caused by any direct atmospheric causes, such as atmospheric pressure, than by simple lights and colour-effects.

The angle of reflection need not necessarily be equal to the angle of incidence, as the surface of the cloud may or may not be a horizontal reflecting plane. And, under varying directions and circumstances of the wind-drift across the sun and the formation of the clouds, or at night across the sky and moon, so will these combined effects of light vary, whether natural or artificial. Hence the varieties of weathers, lights, and effects which we endeavour to describe further on.

Thus, according to whether the plane of the reflecting surfaces be horizontal, as in

A B, or at the other angles shown in the
accompanying diagrams, viz., at the angles
to the planes of C-D or E-F or G-H or
L-K, so will the angle of reflection O M N
be equal, or greater, or less than the angle
of incidence L M O.

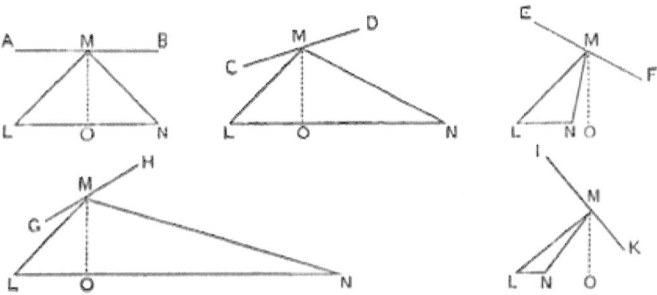

And further, if the plane of the reflecting
surfaces be corrugated or uneven, the more
conflicting and numerous will be the many
different angles of reflection, and the colours
of sky and reflected lights become more and
more fatal to the angler's hopes of success.
And we believe also the direct rays of sunlight, making many angles with the plane of
the stream surface, or the bed of the river, or
particular reaches of the river, at different
hours of the day, have also varying effects
upon the feeding, or upon the vision of trout.

We are not going to enter into more complicated subjects such as the angles of *refracted* rays of light passing through the denser medium of water. But we cannot help thinking that purely natural causes may yet be discovered for the phenomena connected with the surface-feeding of trout and salmon.

In the same way, and we believe for similar reasons, or arising from similar effects of light and reflected light, night-fishing for trout is rarely, or never, so successful on moonlight nights, and the best nights for fly-fishing are dark nights—not necessarily dark, however, from cloudy sky. Besides this, as we elsewhere point out, it is often on such dark nights *that a black fly kills best.*

In a recently published volume of the *Fur, Feather, and Fin* series—on Salmon—an account is given of a remarkable day's salmon-fishing, which we consider worthy of reproduction in this connection, when all the hours at which each fish was hooked were noted down — an experience which finds hundreds of parallels in all salmon anglers' memories or registers. We have also for many years noted down similar records in our Salmon Registers, and we will quote two instances out of many as extremes :—

The example from *Fur, Feather, and Fin* series (p. 119) is as follows, as related in tabular form :—

During the first hour and fifty minutes— 10.5 A.M. to 11.55—*eight* fish were *brought to net* out of *nine* hooked.

In the next period of same length of time —12.10 to 2 P.M.—*seven* fish out of *nine* were *lost*.

Then between 2.10 and 5.50 *ten* fish out *eleven* were brought to net.

It is further interesting to read the Hon. Gathorne-Hardy's notes ; but while granting that such experiences are quite common, as all anglers know, he does not attempt to explain the cause.

We will now supplement the above with one of many experiences of our own :—

On the 14th July 1896 we had a lively experience on the Upper Inver.

Began at Neck at 11 A.M. Rose one shy twice by 11.20.

Next pool—Narrows—11.30. Hooked, and at once lost one at far tail.

Small Holes—Narrows—11.45. Lightly touched and lost a good fish.

Black Pool—Narrows. At 12 noon rose a good fish short at top; came and turned with his mouth shut, very short. Immediately after, at 12.15, we hooked, played, and landed a pretty little fish (8 lbs.), covered with sea-lice.

Minister's Pool. At 12.50 had on a jiggering fish and lost him. This pool did not *look* in A 1 order.

Washing Pool. Drew blank, *too low*.

Minister's Pool (second time over). Yanked, as we believed, hard—and of purpose—into a nice fish, and had him on; but in five minutes he came to the top, jiggered, splashed, shook his head and was gone.

Lunched 1.30. Then :—

Black Pool (second time over). Rose one again very short, the fly passing over his head and shoulders. Would not come again.

Neck, 3 P.M. Rose one short, killed another, a small grilse, 5 lbs.

Fished all the Narrows over again, and then Deer Pool down from road-side. Saw nothing more. All the upper pools (Grasseys, Lochanneaski, etc.) useless—*too low*, and Washing Pool and Deer Pool *ditto*.

I used a small 'black doctor' all the time, and I did *not* take my flies away from the fish, having a perfectly cool head at that work after some twenty-five years' experience of that river. On other occasions on the Inver similar experiences could be accounted for by a strong *up-stream* wind bellying one's line, whilst one was obliged to stand high above the pools—witness Red Pool and the next below—but on the day above related there was no adverse wind, but the day was bright and somewhat electrical, with 'big bad clouds,' and after 3 became worse, when they would not move at all.

These two instances illustrate the best rising between 10 and 12. The slack time between 12 and 2, and again a good time between 2.10 and 5.50 in the first case; and in the second case a continuous rising of fish, but slack and short and uncertain, 11 to 3, except two at 12.15 and 3. After 3 nothing, and trap came about 5.20 P.M. to take us up to Inchnadamph.

Often, however, we kill plenty of fish right in the middle of a hot, clear, bright summer day, in low water, *with no clouds*, with a small 'Jock Scott.'

Many parallel instances can be given, as every angler knows, under both salmon and trout; but no one seems to keep careful enough notes as to weathers, barometrical pressures, etc., or light and colour.[1] So far, however, as we have done so with trout, we find such occasions in strict accordance with one another and with atmospheric accompaniments. On such days, also, we have often observed that a smaller class of fish rises, or otherwise large fish in poor condition, though this does not apply to clean, silvery, fresh-run summer salmon. One more remark—when the 'dog-days' come in, this 'short rising' both of salmon, sea trout, and brown trout becomes commoner and commoner. As all know, the 'dog-days' are charged with electricity, and lights and colours are accordingly affected.

---

[1] See light and colour of water and sky reflections, *ante*, under 'Flies,' p. 39.

When a day is hot, sultry, electrical, before the storm bursts fish do not rise well, especially trout; but after a storm or a storm-cloud bursts, and heavy plumps of rain or even hail fall, fish become more lively. This, we believe, is due to two combined causes—the effects of change in the light, and owing also to oxygenation of the water. Salmon are, we believe, really less influenced in these respects than trout.

It would appear that fish do not rove about in search of food in such conditions, but remain, so to speak, 'glued to the bottom'—and both trout and salmon and sea-trout are all affected. Even the net fishermen know this, and may even be observed to take their work easier when such provision is made by the clerk of the weather —say, for instance, on some river pool of Lower Spey in August. It is when fish are running or roving that both net and rod do most among *fresh-run fish*. Fish require to be wakened up from sleep or sulking (?) before they can be expected to take the fly on the surface. So much do we believe this, that we do not consider it a *guilty thing* to *stone a pool* where many 'potted fish' are lying, before fishing it (and we know of angling friends who can bear us out in this statement, with the same personal experiences as ourselves). Of course the unthinking angler may pooh-pooh such an idea, and we don't think there are a preponderating number of even experienced anglers who would enjoy the sight of a small boy playing 'ducks and drakes' over a pet pool; and how often do we hear 'anathemas galore' hurled at the devoted bands of Goosanders or Red-breasted Mergansers and their young, which go 'flafferin'' down through the pools in front of one's cast! If no salmon are seen in these pools, the blame is promptly placed on 'these confounded birds,' which 'ought to be shot.' We do not affirm they may not be to blame in some measure, or at times, but we do believe a 'sulky' pool is not made any worse by it.

At another opportunity, when salmon is more correctly our theme, we may give curious instances in proof of our contention that a lot of sulky fish make a pool sulky, and the fish are none the worse for being wakened out of their sulks (or is it jealousy of one another?)[1]; and of course another factor may be, and probably is, a deficiency in physical energy of these fish, caused by electrical conditions (affecting, as some writer lately put it, the 'condition of their enlarged livers!').

---

[1] Many anglers must have often witnessed what is termed 'moving fish.' Where many are congregated together in a favourite pool, and the salmon-fly passes enticingly over them, one or more, or several of these fish, are 'moved.' Under such circumstances we have persistently *stoned* that pool, and the next time we fished it over we have often taken a fish promptly when the salmon-fly hung over the favourite lie. In this case fear of one another may have been the dominating factor in their unwillingness to rise to the surface.

XI

FOOD-SUPPLIES AND RELEVANT
MATTERS

THE 'times of the take,' we believe, is re-
gulated by general conditions of temperatures of air and water and amount of sun-
heat, and of course upon the consequent
hatch-off of fly. Early in the season the
take may be earlier in the day, *i.e.* before
snow-water has melted or pulsed the river,
and (or) in seasons following a mild winter,
when 'March browns' and 'early duns,' etc.,
have got off. The 'rise' may be as early as
10 A.M., and continue fitfully till 12 or even
till 1; but this latter is exceptional. Nearly
the same occurs if there be a long succession of
high-water levels and cold skies, even if there
be no snow near the sources. In May the feed
comes on the surface, in most seasons sometimes as early as 8 A.M., but more commonly
about 10.30 and most frequently about 11.
But if frost or mist is down, but lifting,

the feed is usually delayed till about midday. If the day gets colder as it advances,
or the sun can't struggle through, there is
little rise at all. But if the day gets milder
and sunnier in the afternoon, some of these
days yield best baskets, even as late as between 1 or 1.30 and 3 or 4 P.M. These are
usually choice days, but they don't occur
very often, and in a bad season hardly
ever.

In summer the rise or tid may continue
longer, even from early morning to late.
Still, the most 'business' can usually be
transacted from about 8 to 3, and then again in
the evening. There is rarely an evening rise
in April or May, even on the livelier broken
water. (We speak of northern rivers!)

Why trout often take in a hailstorm in
April or May, or later if such occurs, we
believe to be because the water becomes
oxygenated, the electric disturbance before-
hand emphasising the change—this and
the drowned-fly food together. In the same
way the livelier the water the livelier the
fish, and on the lower and deader reaches of
a river like Don and Deveron, trout 'go off'
sooner than on higher reaches of the same.

The run of elvers or small eels takes place in May, varying with different seasons. We believe this to prove a great 'stodge' for trout, and after it takes place trout for some time do not rise nor feed steadily on fly, even when fly is abundant on the surface. This movement of elvers usually takes place between the 10th and 15th of May (in the Deveron at least). In 1894 they ran on the 13th and 14th, with a rising water and north-east wind, as was witnessed by a number of residents; and at various localities we have ourselves seen them about the same period. A full flood followed the run of 1894, and trout were completely down after that on the lower reaches of the Deveron, but continued livelier about twelve miles higher up, at Rothiemay, for about a week or ten days later. We are not inclined to put this 'going off feed' to the flood and popular reason—a gorge of worms—because a few trout we got were not gorged with worms, but with eels, larvæ, caddis. One in particular seemed to have eaten nothing but eels. And worm-fishing, at least, had not begun.

In the same way a gorge of caddis and

larvæ, or of stonefly and creeper, fed upon by what the fishing papers term 'tailers,' produces a similar cessation from surface food, but scarcely lasting so long as an elver stodge. Worm we never consider has a similar 'stodging' effect, or if so only for a very short time, for one reason, viz., trout principally take to worm after they attain to their best fly condition, or again after they have been luxuriating in elvers. They do feed on worms at all times more or less; but a day or two, or indeed a few hours, in a flood feeding on green worms suffices for them. We cannot believe that green worms feed or satisfy or improve the muscular condition of fish as fly does, and green worms in a spate are bound to scour the fish more than to feed them. Perhaps we might find in worm a natural provision of nature as a blood-purifier and purge for trout, as green grass is taken by a dog for a vomit.

We usually find that large trout are seldom in equal condition—*i.e.* as regards shape and firmness of flesh—to small trout in the same river, and this lack of condition extends far into the season; indeed, rarely are big trout

—*i.e.* trout far above the average—in as eatable condition as the smaller ones.

We believe this is accounted for by the comparative ages of the trout: on the one hand, the juvenile smaller trout—or, so to speak, the grilse of the trout—which have never spawned, and on the other the older adult trout which *have* spawned, and which take longer to recover from their winter kelted condition of muscle. Indeed, it is more than possible the young fish may not have severely lost condition all winter. (See our remarks under 'Comparison and History of Seasons,' *infra*, p. 108).

Also we find parallel conditions amongst the young of the migratory *Salmonidae*, such as the famed (or notorious ? !) finnocks of the north-east of Scotland—Ythan, Dee, Deveron, Spey, Findhorn, etc. etc.—or the unspawned grilse of the sea-trout of March and April. These descend the rivers of the east coast about the same time that the run of elvers takes place, and many of these young sea-trout, which are caught in the estuaries, are what may be termed 'weel-mended' after their gorge on the elvers.

Early in March and in April, and even

during part of May, the 'March browns' are abundant, the large lighter ones coming on a little later than the small darker ones—let us say of the same swarm. We give a general preference to the lighter, as we believe the trout do; and often when the darker males (?) are going down like fleets of herring-boats, the female (?) fly makes the basket. Stewart advocates a smaller imitation than the natural insect. We do *not* find that advice invariably good.

Geological conditions :—

A friend who has studied the question of the influences of geological conditions upon trout and trout food, and one who has had abundant and continuous opportunities both as an angler and one of the staff of the Scottish Geological Survey, reports to us as follows :—'My impression is, the condition of trout depends almost entirely upon the abundance of fly food; and as the hatching out of the river flies is mainly dependent on temperatures of air and water, geological conditions only indirectly influence condition of the fish.' Mr Hinxman continues :—' The trout in a limestone district are well fed owing to the amount of crustacea—gammari, etc.—and I remember the trout in the chalk streams of Wiltshire were often in good condition by the end of March. Streams flowing through " drift-covered " country like the Don are again likely to be earlier than those in which there is much bare rock and shifting shingle channel; but I do not think that, with the exception of limestone and chalk, the nature of the rock makes much difference. Elevation, temperatures, and snow-water are probably the chief factors.' Illustrative of this, and speaking of the very cold, bleak May of 1898, he adds :—' This has been a very cold, bleak season, and such few trout as there are here (he is writing from a locality high up in Lochaber), have been very late of getting into condition, while there has been hardly any fly to speak of, though red-spinners were out on the —— Burn in pretty large numbers on the 23rd May. I suspect you have not done so well on the Deveron as usual.' (See our ' Comparison and History of Seasons,' *ante,* p. 105.)

That seasonal changes take place in fish at different times and even among different individuals in the same stream is a well-known yet interesting fact. To illustrate this let us offer a few examples. In May 1894 a trout was killed and opened by us at the river-side. It was full of ova in strings about the size of snipe-shot. This trout was about half a pound, and in prime condition. Others were afterwards found in a similar interesting state. In July, from a high-level loch in Sutherland, Loch Gorm, which is much fed by snow-wreaths on the north-east face of Ben More, Assynt, we found many *pink-*, or almost *red-*fleshed trout full of ova the size of seed-pearls, and, notwithstanding the rich colour of the flesh, flabby and 'cotton-woolly' when cooked.

Again, on April 8th, 1897, a 'baggit' salmon was hooked and landed. There were ripe, large handsome ova running from her in our presence. A gentle pressure, however, produced no more. She had dashed at and taken a spinning bait, and she was kelted in shape. She must have deposited the principal portion of her ova just before she took that Devon minnow. Our landlord, the laird of the water we were fishing, himself an experienced salmon-fisher, pronounced it as 'one of these late-running fish of last year!' We confess not perfectly to understand it.[1]

Again, in the upper waters of the Endrick —a Stirlingshire stream—on the 1st September we found trout running both milt and ova so universally that we stopped fishing. Yet on many lochs and rivers trout are perfectly fit to kill and eat in September, and even in some (lochs, at least) as late as October. At St. Fillans, on Loch Earn, we have caught trout which were perfectly good on the table in October, when, at the same time, on the small tributaries of Ruchil Water, we found trout pushing their noses upon the edges of the 'divots' and among the grassy runlets—full of spawn.

Dark-red salmon still pushing up as spawners were caught by rod on the Oich in March 1898, which could scarcely have

[1] But we look upon this instance as a proof that a salmon which had evidently only just completed her spawning operations dashed hungrily at the Devon minnow. It would have been interesting to have dissected this fish and observed the condition of her stomach, in connection with the question of 'salmon *feeding* in fresh water.' (See Fishery Board Report, Blue Book, 1898.)

left the sea and entered the Ness later than
the previous November—*i.e.* if they had ever
been down to salt water at all! But as a
curious companion instance to this, a single
specimen of the so-called *Salmo Killinensis*
of Gunther, or the char of Loch Killin above
the Falls of Foyers, was caught by worm
in the tidal part of the river Ness early
in March 1898 (vide *Annals of Scottish
Natural History,* April 1898). Strange
that—escaping from Loch Killin into Loch
Ness—this fish should not descend below
the layer of spate-water in Loch Ness,
but find its way down three-fourths of the
whole length of the loch, as if making
willingly to the sea !

Many more curious instances could be
given, and it might be worth the trouble
some day to collect such facts for future
use, both with a bearing upon their natural
conditions of life and changes of diet, and
also as possible influences to guide legislation
when framing an Act for a close-time for trout.

We certainly want a close-time for trout,
but we require the same to be suited to
innumerable conditions, and to each river

or group of rivers, under their own climatal conditions and temperatures and seasons, and other physical and natural conditions of late and early rivers. (We purpose returning to the subject of close-times, poaching, and illegal fishing later on.)

Sheep drains and general drainage of river slopes. — This is perhaps a fruitful cause of deterioration in size of trout, and in diminution of numbers, and Stewart speaks at length regarding it, and is most accurate in his remarks (pp. 23, 24), and we do not deem it necessary to dilate upon the subject, as such would, for the most part, be 'harping on a very old tune,' except to say that such rivers as are less subjected to this artificial drainage are usually found—other advantages being included—to be the best trout streams. A river, for instance, that is dependent upon deep-set and innumerable springs, and which is not dependent upon flood-water *only* for its bulk and flow, will maintain an even flow and a better standard as a trouting river than one which is subjected to continuous spates of surface washings, and even than one which has large

series of reservoirs or lochs at the head
waters. Where a 'medium' stage of water
can run longest, becoming 'amber' and even
'clear,' and keep such 'medium' or first
stages of 'low' levels for the greatest time,
these rivers are the most reliable for sport
and a good average size of trout. (We do
not bring in here any direct reference to
artificial spates, or dams sluiced to bring up
the migratory *salmonidæ*. That appears
to us to be a totally different matter.)

Now, talking of the averages of killable
trout, we have always considered that as
much pure enjoyment can be got out of
some mountain burn or rocky stream, where
the average is known to be, say, a quarter-
pound, or even where the average is known
rarely to exceed six to the pound, and where
an angler can make a trim little basket of
ten or twelve pounds by *careful* and *scientific*
angling with fly or worm. We are ourselves perfectly happy—happier, indeed, with
smaller fish, than when, upon lower, more
sluggish reaches, it may be, of the same river,
hours are spent over the obtaining of a rise,
except during the short 'time of the take,

lasting possibly half an hour only (and where in that time the rise is certainly fast and furious), and when the same weight of trout may be basketed with bigger fish. The average—say half-pound to three-quarters of a pound—is better, but the sport is not so continuous nor so pleasing, nor at the end of a day does one look back upon it as so satisfactory. We know many anglers differ from us, and prefer the big fish. For our own part, we never consider, at least on a Scottish stream, that a quarter-pound trout is too small to basket, even where the average of a whole basketful be found to be the half-pound (there are plenty of that size in the stream). But the true average of a stream ought to be considered at that which it produces when its best average trout are feeding, and quarter-pound trouts (where the average runs from, say, three to the pound or the half-pound, or in exceptional seasons closely approaches three-quarters) *ought* to be basketed, but nothing under that weight.

In the river Fiddich, a tributary of Spey, the trout average about five or six to the pound. Knowing this, many a lovely day

we have spent upon it before the distilleries
became upon its banks almost as numerous
as 'black beetles' in a yellow flood![1]

But how many local fishermen are there
who turn back into the water all the *par,
small trout*, or large, lanky, ill-conditioned
fish they catch? If they are down-stream
fishers in low, clear, summer water, *very*
often they would come home 'clean' if they
did. One local fisher we wot of, who was
found drowned in shallow water, having
tripped and fallen in on his face, who locally
was looked upon as a 'king among fishers,'
who kept a record of the *numbers only* of
the fish he killed, and in a lifetime scored
some thousands and thousands, bagged every-
thing he 'yanked' out, from par up to, say, a
few odd pounders, and always selected the
narrow bit burns and smaller streams in
order to increase his *tale*.

Under circumstances of summer waters
low and clear, when up-stream anglers have
met with a favourable day and up-stream
breeze, or a cool, drizzly day in June or July,
and come in with baskets of seven, eight, or

---

[1] See Table showing measurements and weights of
trout in good condition and in bad condition, p. 137 *infra*.

ten pounds or more, *several* down-streamers
with poles—'far-off fishers'—have returned
with pocket, poke, or basket of *par*! and often
with only a few miserable trout of ounces.

We don't grudge them *their* 'sport'—far
from it; but we do object to be denounced
as we once were, to our knowledge, thus:—
'Oh, I know these *gentlemen*' (we were
pleased at this saving clause) 'were fishing
with salmon roe. I know it. They could
not kill these trout any other way,' with vain
repetitions harping on the same miserable
and jealous chord. The date was midsummer, the river low — 0.0.0. of scale
(*q.v.*). We cannot therefore accuse the de-
tractor of '*Honi soit que mal y pense.*'
'Gentleman (?) of the salmon-roe-persuasion,'
please tell our readers if salmon roe is a good
lure under these circumstances, or, failing
knowledge on that point, please tell them
whether it is a killing bait in Spey, say
around Rothes or Aberlour, 'earlier or
later in the season in a drumly water!'
Only once having used it in our life, and
then 'jist for the raal curiosity o' the thing'
—and not at midsummer—we are not in a
position to educate as regards it.

When we did use it we felt inclined to break our rod as not likely ever again to be successful in honest and gentlemanly sport. I think *now*, that rod must be where all bad rods go, and that it has been there now for at least thirty years. But this by the way.

Process of population, and dispersal of insect life in a stream.—Take the 'March brown,' hatching out in March and April, and in higher reaches even all summer and into August ('August dun'). The fly floats down stream, cock-winged in flotillas. The females lay their eggs on the surface, and die. Eggs reach the bottom in time, and in correct season and in normal seasons hatch-off and become larvæ. Later, they pass upward again to the surface, reaching the surface with the current, and become male and female 'March browns,' or various shades of that well-known insect. Again the females float down stream, lay eggs, and die.

Given that the above is correct so far, there is evident tendency to populate reaches lower down than those where the winged insect deposited its ova.

But if a wind blows up the river, or up any reaches of it, the females and males are drifted by the wind higher up the river from the place of their first appearance, and alighting on the surface lay their eggs.

Given this is also correct, then the other tendency is so far counterbalanced.

The Grannom fly has been successfully introduced and hatched-off on a river in England (Berkshire), and it 'appears to have gone somewhat lower down the river than where the eggs were located, etc.'—(*Fishing Gazette*, April 23rd, 1898.)

'*Tailing of trout*' (so much written about in sporting papers) is a well-known habit of trout when feeding on larvæ. We witness this more and more in later years, but we cannot say we have noticed any corresponding decrease of insect food on the surface. We can, however, 'jalouse' (Anglicé, suspect; Yankee, 'guess') that where dry-fly fishing is 'all the rage,' trout may get sick of stinging insects, and more and more take to 'ruttling' in the mud and slime like pigs. We cannot say that this habit seems to be dependent on weather, or water, or temperature. It may occur at almost any time, especially during a long drought. It is equally certain it occurs when rivers are running high, as can easily be proved by a slight examination of such trout as may vary their method of feeding, and be caught by an artificial fly at such times.

Trout taking in a hailstorm.—This may arise, as we have already said, simply because of the *drowned* fly, or it may be caused by change from sultry weather and tepid water, reoxygenated by the pattering of the hail or rain-shower.

Trout not taking before rain.—Unless before the rain there are electrical conditions of the atmosphere, we do not place entire confidence in this old saw. If the water be otherways oxygenated, as by rapid streams, or broken water, or under a fall, trout often take well before rain-showers. If the weather be setting down for a regular wet day, *then* trout may not do well before it commences, but when this occurs, say in June or July, as a rule there are electric and barometric causes combined. Sometimes, we have certainly noticed, before heavy rain a smaller class of trout come on the feed; or otherwise we catch ill-conditioned fish. This, as we have tried to explain before, seems to us a sure indication that the average or larger and best-conditioned trout are down, and the younger, more active ones are getting a chance to feed, and take advantage of it; while larger but imperfect-conditioned fish also take the chance given by the refusal of their stronger neighbours.

There are many bad days when only *small* or badly fed trout are found to be on the move, and thus we account for it. We feel pretty sure we are not far wrong, as we make our analyses and averages pretty carefully.

Trout feel warm or cold in the hand when taken out of the water.—This, surely, almost all anglers must have noticed, and on those days when they feel cold, *i.e.* colder than human-blood temperature, it is usually (we think we are correct) when the temperature of the air is very much warmer than that of the water, and usually on such days they do not rise well.

Temperatures of air and water.—We have rarely found trout rise well when the following temperatures are found to rule (and we here refer our readers to our Tables, showing some of these rulings, and to the Tables which illustrate day-to-day records, which are taken direct from our regular fishers' registers).

GOOD SPRING BASKETS

Date and Hours of Take.	Weather. Temperatures of Water. Temperatures of Air. Barometer.	State of River or Loch. High° Med.° Low°	Wind. Up Down	Anglers' Names or Initials.	Trout Caught. No.	Wgt.	Condition	Av.	Flies or Lures.	Name of River or Loch and County.
Ap. 16, 1894.	Temperatures not read. Morning mist till 9.30. Trout rose tardily, 10.30. Intervals: furious, 11.45 to 12.30. Not a move, 3 to 4.30.	0 0	s. to E. up.	J.A.H.B.	15	10	Fair.		Mar. brown. Greenwell. Early brown.	Drachlaw.
Ap. 24, 1894.	Air 45°, water 47° at 10 a.m. „ 50°, „ 52 at 5 p.m. Hard.	0 0 0 but clear.	E. up.	J.R.W.C.	23	10½			Mar. brown.	Netherdale.
Ap. 22, 1896.	Temperatures not read. Warm, mist and drizzle, to heavy mist and rain. 10.30 to 2 p.m. and till 3 p.m.	0	E. to N.E.	J.A.H.B.	18	11½	Good. one at one at	2 lbs. 1¾ lbs.	Grey quill.	Turnwheel Reach.
Ap. 7, 1897.	Air 50°, water 42° at noon. Cloudy; warmer than all the weeks before. Rise on in the afternoon.	0 0 0 but clear.	s. to S.E.	A.F.	42	23¾	Poor.	2 lbs.	Greenwell. Early dun. Mar. brown.	Laithers Haugh.
Ap. 12, 1897.	Air 50°, water 42° at 9.30. Cloudy, SSE. 1.30 to 2.30.	0 0 0 pulsing snow.	s.s.E. down.	A F. (all day) J.A.H.B. (1 hour).	34 13	16½ 8	Fair. one at Poor.	2 lbs.	Small Greenwell Red quill.	Laithers Haugh and down.
Ap. 22, 1898.	Air 48°, and at 3, 50°. Water , at 3 p.m., 54°. Mist on water rose off by 9.31. Frost in morning. Sun came out at 12. Rise 12.30 to 1.15.	0 0 clear.	s. to S.E.	J.A.H.B.	13	8	Good.		Mar. brown. Saltoun. Hare's ear.	Upper Heron and Drachlaw.

The above are selected to show good spring days and baskets, but observe: the fish are hungry and in poor condition on the earlier dates.

BAD SPRING BASKETS

Date and Hours of Take.	Weather. Temperatures of Water. Temperatures of Air. Barometer.	State of River or Loch. High° Med° Low°	Wind. Up Down N.E. S.W.	Anglers' Names or Initials.	Trout Caught. No.	Wgt	Condition	Av.	Flies or Lures.	Name of River or Loch and County.
Apr. 21, 1894.	Air 52°, water 51° 10 a.m. „ 49°, „ 54°, 1 p.m. „ 47°, „ 54°, 4 p.m. Dry, hard, cold, gusty.	00	S.E. up	J.R.C. J.A.H.B. did not fish	4	2¾	Fair.		?	Laithers.
Apr. 27, 1894.	Air 51°, water 54° 10 a.m. „ 52°, „ 56°, 4 p.m. Hard, glittering sky; plenty of fly, but no rise.	00	E.	J.R.C.	5	2½			Mar. brown. Hare's lug.	Laithers. Heron Pool.
Apr. 28, 1896.	Air 46°, water 50°, 9 a.m. Dark, heavy, thundery, but cold. Not a rise till afternoon. Hailstorm when 3 were got.	00	W.	J.A.H.B.	3	2½	one	1¼	Grey quill.	Drachlaw.
Apr. 13, 1897.	Air 45°, water 44°, noon. Fearful cold, gloomy, dark. A.F. blown off by 3 p.m.	000 rising	S.S.E.	A.F.	12	5	Good.		?	Laithers.
Apr. 18, 1898.	Air and water not taken. Bitter cold gale. Uniform dark-leaden sky.	00	E.	J.A.H.B. 3 hours.	2	1			Mar. brown. Broughton point.	{ Drachlaw and Upper Heron.
Apr. 21, 1898.	Air 52°!! 9 a.m. „ 62°!!! 2.30 p.m. Water 44°!! 10 a.m. „ 52°!!! 2.30 p.m. Lovely sky.	00	gentle S.E.	J.A.H.B.	7	3¼	Bad.		Mar. brown (large).	{ Laithers. Turnwheel Reach.

The above days are descriptive of early spring bad days, and results of full days' fishing, different years. The last is remarkable re temperatures.

GOOD MAY BASKETS

Date and Hours of Take.	Weather. Temperatures of Water. Temperatures of Air Barometer.	State of River or Loch. High ° Med. ° Low °	Wind. Up — Down	Anglers' Names or Initials.	No.	Wgt.	Condition	Av.	Flies or Lures.	Name of River or Loch and County.
May 1, 1894.	Temperatures not read. Cold, dark, showery up to 1 p.m.; not a rise. Then lighter; less wind; warmer all afternoon. Few flies on—duns.	0 up 2″	N.W. up on Mid. Heron. N.E. S.W.	J.A.H.B. Fished 10.30 to 1. Fished 1 to 4 p.m.	31	19 best 1¾	A 1		Greenwell. Hare's lug.	Two lower Herons.
May 3, 1894.	Forenoon—brisk, steady, dull; roving clouds; good. Afternoon—changed to cold; heavy cold rains; blustery. Bad. Veered 11 to 12.30.		w.	J.A.H.B. Fished 11 to 2.30.	15	8½	A 1	3/4	Greenwell. Grey quill. Do., small.	Drachlaw. Haugh.
May 5, 1894.	Forenoon—bad, cold, dark; fiery glints; no rise on. Afternoon—warmer; no wind; front lost on glides, sunk-fly.	0	N.W. to 0 to E.	J.A.H.B.	19	10½	A 1	1¼	Greenwell. Grey quill. Woodcock and Yellow.	Herons.
May 2, 1896.	Air 50°, water 48°, 9 a.m. Warmer: dull; cloudy; little sun.	00 Black after flood.	N.N.W. up.	J.A.H.B.	18	13	A 1		Professor. Orange Greenwell.	Laithers. Lowest beat.
May 6, 1897.	Temperatures not read. Weather variable; sky broken; squalls with hail: almost a gale. Then dead calm and warm. By 5.30 mild : by night balmy.	Low 0 0	N.W. down.	J.A.H.B.	18	9 best 1½ lbs.	A 1		Dun. Wee J. S. Snipe and purple.	Drachlaw.

The above are samples of May baskets.

BAD MAY BASKETS

Date and Hours of Take.	Weather. Temperatures of Water. Temperatures of Air. Barometer.	State of River or Loch. High°/Med.°/Low°	Wind. Up/Down. N.E./S.W.	Anglers' Names or Initials.	Trout Caught. No.	Wgt.	Con-dition.	Av.	Flies or Lures.	Name of River or Loch and County.
May 7, 1894.	Electric, thundery, fiery, 10 a.m. Blizzard of hail, gowk storm, 10.30 a.m. Hot and cold, calm and wind, alternating all day. Trout rising short.	A 1	0 up flawy	J.A.H.B.	10	4½	'so-so.'	¾	Greenwell's Glory. Professor. Woodcock and Yellow.	R. Deveron. Netherdale.
May 8, 1894.	S. wind, criss-cross, flawy. Cold, heavy rain.	Drumly 000		J.R.W.C. J.A.H.B.	8	4			,,	Drachlaw.
May 22, 1894.	Glare, glitter, white clouds. Down-stream wind. Trout rising short.	High 000	N.E. down	J.R.W.C. J.A.H.B.	3 2	1½? 2½?		1 lb.	Part. and Orange.	Laithers.
May 1, 1895.	Air, 9 a.m., 52°, water 51°. Bright, glittery, bad clouds. Half gale down stream.	0 0		J.R.W.C. J.A.H.B.	3 2	14 oz. ½ lb.			Mar. brown. Greenwell's Glory.	Laithers.
May 2, 1895.	Air 45°, water 45°, 9 a.m. Water black. Not a trout seen rising till 12.30. Then only small.			J.R.W.C. J.A.H.B.	5 6	3½ 2½			Professor. Orange hackle.	Laithers.
May 11, 1898.	Air 44°, water 46°, 9 a.m. Cold, dark, rain, gale. Barometer away down.			Did not fish.	*Experientia docet.*					
May 14, 1898.	Air 47°, water 47°, 8.45 a.m. 46°, 11.20 a.m. Air 49°, ,, 2 p.m.	High 000		Did not fish.	Hopeless.					Laithers.

Indeed we had scarcely any good days in May 1898 for reasons already given.

ILLUSTRATIONS OF GOOD AND BAD DAYS.

The History of a Day: Deveron.

(Take two consecutive days, 21st and 22nd
April 1898.)

April 21*st.*—Rapid changes of temperature—

Air, 52° at 9 A.M., and 62° by 2.30.

Water, 44° at 10 A.M., and 52° by 2.30.

Now, what would we expect? Little, and
we won't be disappointed !

A sudden change of air temperature,

But a slow change of water temperature.

We fished from 10.30 to 1 P.M. Had four
rises and killed two trout. These two trout
were lanky, poor, and black. They were
taken when the air was 52° and the water
46°. There seemed little to find fault with
in the sky or weather. A marbled sky and
faint east to south-east wind. Water still
full (0 0 of scale), and amber (or clear, *not*
crystal). Early creepers seen—a few.

After lunch at 1, fished till 3.30 P.M. Got
one more in Wheel, two on Heron, two on
Drachlaw. Flies were 'March brown' and
' Broughton point.'

Argument.

When water is at about its coldest, and the air makes a jump, only ill-conditioned fish rise, or small, and when the air leaves the water in the lurch by 10° all day. On such days possibly some small trout may rise, and such may be—

'Capable, keepable, eatable,
  Excellent, esculent, succulent.'

April 22nd.—Frost in the morning, and frost-mist down on the water, but gradually rising to top of hill.

At 10 A.M. air 48°, water not taken.

At 3 P.M. air 50°, water 54°.

Before going out I prophesied to myself, 'Trout won't take till midday, and not then unless the sun comes out.'

I began at 10.30 and got four *small* trout by 12. At Heron I sat down and smoked a pipe. This brought me to 12.20. Sun gleams came out at 12. Smash of trout on—'early dun.' Between 12.20 and 1.20 I killed thirteen trout (8 lbs.), but not another rise. They hooked badly, and of the thirteen six were hooked foul.

Came in to lunch.

Went out again at 2. I had come in as the trout had entirely ceased to move after 1.20. Half a gale of wind, east. Heavy wave up Drachlaw Pool. Steely brazen sky, and by 7 P.M. *air temperature* down to 46°. Of course I never saw a fin.

Take now the history of a good day, and in May.

Temperatures not taken, but following noted.

May 1*st*, 1894.—Fished 10.30 to 1, and 1.30 to 4 P.M. Cold, dark, showery up to 1 P.M. *Not a rise.* Then lighter, warmer, all afternoon; but *few* flies on the water, the time of the hatch-off being over (usually 10.30 to 12, or so). But a few nice trout seen rising 'to themselves.'

Water low (0 of scale), wind north-west, and *up* on the Mid-Heron bends.

Fished again 1.30 to 4 P.M., and trout were still rising when I had my basket full. Thirty-one trout, 19 lbs. (I thought I had 20 lbs.). Best trout, 1¾ lbs. Fly, 'Greenwell's glory.'

On this day the change for the better took place after midday (see above). By that time fly-hatch was over, but trout took sure and deadly.

Having given one or two tables of the histories of days, we will now give

ILLUSTRATIONS OF SEASONS.

1. A season of extreme drought and heat.
2. A season of great cold, and rain, and dark heavy water, after a mild February and March.

1. *The History of a Season,* 1893.

In 1893 we arrived at our fishing quarters on Deveron on May 2nd.

There had at that time been five weeks of dead-low water (0.0.0.0. of scale). Longest set of low-level records. This state of affairs lasted in all ten weeks from the time the drought began—up to the 22nd June. We had some five miles of water to fish by permission, and rented two more, for May, for two rods.

On the 6th.—Bright; strong wind making waves up; roving sky, low, clear to crystal water. One rod, twenty-five trout, 10 lbs.

On the 8th.—Bar. 30°; bright sun; few clouds; wind east, up.   Twenty-nine trout, 10½ lbs., *one rod.*

After that almost nothing, except on 20th May—twenty-two trout, 9 lbs. (with worm and Stewart tackle; two, small, with fly).

The weather continued sultry and thunderous. By May 15th the river was at its lowest on record since 1826, as vouched for by local residents.

Slime on the stones and channel all the time we were there. Dearth of river flies. Much destroyed in larval stage by the exposure of the channel and river-bed; and could not hatch off in mid-stream for thick coating of slime. All the water springwater, but unfortunately thermometers not used. Many kelts dying of fungus. Trout also beginning to show disease. *But* all this time, and up to 17th May, and as far up as the higher reaches of the river—say 1000 to 1500 feet (as we ascertained from a fellow-angler of scientific carefulness, L. Hinxman of the Geological Staff)—trout were in the PINK OF CONDITION. They were seen 'ruttling' like swine amongst the larvæ and slime, 'standing on their heads' and waving their tails, the latter both under and above water. No wonder they are fat, guzzling at the imprisoned larvæ and caddis !

On the 20th May the river *rose* just one inch by gauge, and between 10.30 and 11.30 we got (one rod) 6¼ lbs. out of one stream, two fish with fly and twelve with worm. On the 22nd June (we left our lower quarters after the 31st May, and by this time had gone to the higher reaches forty miles higher up) a slow, slight rise of river. With that rise a very early run of sea-trout and very small grilse ascended the river Avon as far up as Inchrory. Fresh run sea-trout had never been seen up there so early before. Both sea-trout and grilse were very small—evidently under-fed in the sea or tidal-water. Grilse ran from 1½ to 2½ or 3 lbs.

The barometer had gone down steadily from Monday 11th June, but rain held off till the 22nd. Then the rise of from 18″ to two feet of river came slowly after thirty-six hours rain, and then went slowly back again to the old condition of things.

I

And now trout began very early to go off colour and lose condition. This was quite a month before their time in normal seasons. An almost similar state of affairs held good well into July, and then, on 13th July, bitterly cold, dark and misty, and north wind, and no improvement in fishing.

The above illustration is what we consider the most extraordinary anomalous season in our experience and actual practice on the Deveron. We have known of other seasons perhaps equally uncommon, but on these occasions we think we have not been trout-fishing, but salmon-fishing.

Now, if a succession of similar seasons to 1893 occurred[1]—exceeding drought from March to June and July—trout, while perhaps getting more surface-food than in a cold season and high water (such as 1898 *q.v.*), would nevertheless be forced in large measure to feed upon the larval stages of the insects. One half of the propagating ground

---

[1] ' Blazing sun and blasting blight,
    Tin-pot brazen vault of blue,
  River low and colour light,
    Scum and dirt too floating through.'

of the water-insects being laid bare to the scorching sun is lost. The other half, into which the trout of double the area are crowded, and the larvæ being glutted up in slime, are fed upon voraciously; and most likely few reach maturity or hatch-off at all. The trout get into pink of condition (we never saw them finer on the table), but as rapidly appear to go off colour. It seems evident that larval forms are not so sustaining to trout muscle as winged fly, because even before the summer months were ended, many turned dark in our baskets in a short time.

A succession of such seasons, we believe, would do enormous damage to the feeding capabilities of a stream. In unoxygenated or half stagnant ponds or lakes, such as Presmennan in Haddington, the fish died, and the water became fœtid and covered with a green slime on the surface. Also, in this connection: it is well known Lochleven fishes best in cool seasons and in east winds, because the steady breezes off the sea aerate and oxygenate the otherwise sluggish water. East and north-east winds are the salvation of Lochleven's healthy conditions.

2. *The History of a Season*, 1898.

As a perfect antithesis to the last example we take the season of 1898.

In 1898 we found our water at a medium height, or 0 0 of scale, but dark and cold and inky, with cold water temperature and warmer air, and the water pulsing slightly up and down the gauge. Previous to this the weather had been genial and mild all February and March, and indeed during the previous winter.

Then after the 8th April, and as the season advanced, both air and water became colder, and soon trout went decidedly off condition. Before this they were in better condition than by the middle of May—at least all those which were over three-quarters of a pound or one pound. *Young fish were quite good.*

March browns had appeared early, but afterwards very few were seen, and only one day after the 8th April. Only one day also was a *flight* of early duns seen after the 8th, though a few were seen occasionally; that flight only lasted for a short half-hour, and after it was over the trout took savagely for a short time. But the sky was bad, and they came short. We had six out of thirteen foul-hooked, and pricked and lost more. During all May less and less fly to be seen, unless a few 'iron duns,' black gnats, and a few 'Yellow Sallys.' Even the iron duns—a cold-weather fly—were scarcer than usual, and we killed with the imitation!—(Anglers will know what that signifies.)

We had *temperature of water* recorded between 42° (but colder before that when our thermometers were not in evidence) and to 50° by the middle of May; and of air from 42° and 44° to 56° till the 5th May. Then back again went the readings of both air and water amongst the 40's; skies dark and cold; little or no sun for days and weeks together; no fly 'up'; no rise on; larger trout in poor condition (see measurements and weights). On 26th May air was 46° at 9 A.M. and water 43° at 11.30, and the days often got colder towards midday.

These were combined with hideous weather —dark, bleak, and cold; with high-running water, coloured, and never reaching the low levels at all, getting amber but scarcely ever clear and never crystal. One day only, the 17th May, I am inclined to look upon as a truly lost day. We find it thus described in our Register: 'Probably would have proved a record day, as, although there was a little frost in the morning, it got warmer after midday—first time this year—but alas! both anglers were out of sorts. We saw what we did not see before or since this season, trout rising fast and feeding after 1.30 P.M. Undoubtedly this was a lost day. In the morning water was 47° and remained so, and air had improved from 45° to 50° by 12 o'clock.' After this date, 17th May, trout seemed to go down utterly.

Now we find that we had noted on the 11th April that trout were in 'good condition and quite good on the table,' and 'much forwarder than in 1897' (which was one of our best years on Deveron). Sheriff W—— also, who was fishing Dunlugas water, wrote us that they were in good order, in 'really wonderful order' at that time; and he is not one likely to be led astray in such comparisons. But it was after this they began to show marked deterioration.

The larger fish were in worse condition at the end of May than they were in at the beginning of April.

The markedly thin condition also of a small salmon (*fresh run*), which was taken on the Deveron on 16th May, is also curious. It was excellent to eat and perfectly curdy, but it had not been well fed in the sea whence it came.

The first grilse taken in the nets was at the easternmost net station of the coast on the 21st May, and weighed only one and a half pounds, and only two had been taken at Gordonston, the heavier only weighing three pounds. Continuous gales of north-east wind and roaring surf made net-fishing a failure. We heard of all the returns officially supplied to our landlord, who has taken so much leading interest and cost in having the cruive-dykes removed in the Duff House policies.

Now, in the event of a succession of such seasons as 1898, it seems almost certain that trout would come to feed more and more upon the bottom, on miniature forms of insect-food or other less sustaining items.

But when, as is usually the case, the cold seasons are accompanied by dark skies and a high flooded state of water, it must also appear evident that even the larval food-supply cannot be obtained in sufficient bulk to keep up the condition or size or average of the trout, and deterioration of the stream must ensue. Fortunately Nature does not usually provide such seasons in rapid succession. If she did, we fear the deterioration would assume quite alarming proportions.

MEASUREMENTS AND WEIGHTS OF TROUT IN 1898.

We did not take measures and weights earlier in the season than the dates given below, but, as we have said, the average condition was more nearly approached in April than in May on the lower reaches of the river, and condition decidedly deteriorated as May advanced. Higher up the river in the more rapid water, where more thorough oxygenation had taken place, trout were not in such poor condition, nor does it appear that they lost whatever condition they had attained to.

May 5th, 1 trout measured 18 in., weight 1 lb.

,,	9th, 1	,,	,,	15 ,,	,,	$\frac{3}{4}$,,
,,	10th, 1	,,	,,	16 ,,	,,	1 ,,
,,	10th, 1	,,	,,	14 ,,	,,	1 ,,
,,	14th, 1	,,	,,	14 ,,	,,	1 ,,
,,	14th, 1	,,	,,	14 ,,	under	1 ,,
,,	14th, 1	,,	,,	14 ,,	,,	$\frac{3}{4}$,,
,,	19th, 1	,,	,,	12 ,,	,,	$\frac{3}{4}$,,
,,	19th, 1	,,	,,	12 ,,	,,	$\frac{3}{4}$,,
,,	19th, 1	,,	,,	12 ,,	,,	$\frac{3}{4}$,,
,,	21st, 1	,,	,,	$10\frac{1}{4}$		
,,	21st, 1	,,	,,	$10\frac{1}{2}$	each	$\frac{1}{2}$,,
,,	21st, 1	,,	,,	$11\frac{1}{4}$		
,,	23rd, 1	,,	,,	13 ,,	weight	1 ,,
,,	23rd, 1	,,	,,	$12\frac{1}{2}$,,	under	1 ,,
,,	23rd, 1	,,	,,	12 ,,	weight	$\frac{3}{4}$,,
,,	23rd, 1	,,	,,	11 ,,	,,	$\frac{1}{2}$,,
,,	23rd, 1	,,	,,	10 ,,	nearly	$\frac{1}{2}$,,
,,	25th, 1	,,	,,	$9\frac{1}{2}$,,	weight	6 oz.
,,	25th, 1	,,	,,	9 ,,	,,	4 ,,
,,	25th, 1	,,	,,	$8\frac{1}{2}$,,	,,	$3\frac{3}{4}$,,
,,	27th, 1	,,	,,	11 ,,	,,	11 ,,
,,	27th, 1	,,	. ,,	$10\frac{1}{2}$,,	,,	10 ,,
,,	27th, 1	,,	,,	10 ,,	,,	6 ,,
,,	27th, 1	,,	,,	$8\frac{1}{2}$,,	,,	4 ,,
,,	27th, 1	,,	,,	$7\frac{1}{2}$,,	,,	3 ,,

We wish we had taken many more measurements and weights, and such materials will have our more careful attention in future.

Our measurements and weights are not taken by the ordinary spring-balances, which are often faulty in the smaller weights, and can seldom be relied upon after some time in use, even when specially constructed by a good maker to order—such at least is our own experience many times over.

The following are a few weights sent from Rothiemay under date of 25th May 1898 by an angling friend, along with tracings of outlines of fish.

Rothiemay is fifteen miles by stream higher up the river, but not at a very much greater altitude. The day was rank bad.

May 25th, 1 trout measured $11\frac{1}{4}$ in., wgt. $11\frac{1}{4}$ oz.
„ 25th, 1 „ „ $11\frac{3}{4}$ „ „ $10\frac{1}{2}$ „
„ 25th, 1 „ „ 12 „ „ $10\frac{1}{2}$ „
„ 25th, 1 „ „ $11\frac{1}{4}$ „ „ 9 „

We ought also to mention that our measurements are taken on a straight line between the nose along the medial line to the fork of the tail in all cases.

The following is a specimen of a lanky trout, dating April 18th, 1895 :—

C. H. A. 1 trout measured $19\frac{1}{2}$ in., wgt. 1

lb. 14 oz.; and another for comparison, April 27th, 1896, measured 17½in., wgt. 2 lbs.

Note. — Of course the comparative measurements and weights of trout in condition vary in different streams. All we have given here are of Deveron trout. It is important also, of course, when taking and recording such details, to keep accurate note of the dates; and it might, and we believe would, add to our knowledge if they also tabulated descriptions of the weather at the time they were caught. Those which we have given can be compared with our previous remarks and the other Tables given.

It would be, we think, desirable if a much larger series of measurements and weights for different rivers were recorded in sportmen's registers,[1] and at different seasons—say March, April, May, June, July, and September. Only by a long series of these could positive *scientia* be attained, and much useful data for comparisons be accumulated. We would be pleased to receive such from different rivers with a view to future investigations.

---

[1] Registers, such as we use ourselves, can be obtained from Messrs. Stewart and Co., stationers, George Street, Edinburgh, bound in pads, or in sheets.

XI

TROUTING WITH OTHER DEVICES:
CLOSE TIMES AND POACHING

AMONGST other devices for capturing trout, we merely desire to mention them by name, adding a few remarks here and there.

Green worm in a yellow flood.—Many may think we have said enough or too much already.

Salmon roe is illegal. I done it ' wanst,' but it was not in midsummer!

Snatching is illegal, for salmon. I never done it; but the acts don't work. *The Black Watch-it insec'* often looking on helpless.

Guddling, or 'gunnling,' or 'tickling.' I have. Good fun for a boy, but illegal.

Ottering.—I have done or seen it done twice. Don't see any fun in it. 'Rives' and tears, and renders shy scores of pricked fish:

Illegal, but commonly practised in spite of the law.

Cross - lining. — Illegal and destructive. Never did it, but have seen it done, for both salmon and trout, by a laird and his keeper. (*Game*keeper, I mean.)

Fishing with twelve flies on a cast.— Clyde only, I believe ; *open* water (very) !

Set lines.—Done it—*for eels* or monsters. Never caught many of the latter. Only a few, when one wanted to 'give a loch a fair chance,' when it was ' outwith jurisdiction '; but went on the same principle as the Quaker who said, 'Thou may do it this time, friend, but thou mayst not make a practice thereof.'

Netting.—Have done it once, by permission, to try and reduce an unnecessary stock of small trout in a Highland loch. Party: three 'sportsmen,' six gillies, a pony, and a ' lassie ' looking after the pony. Result: one small trout to each, some boulders, more mud, and a ducking. Didn't try it again !

'*Burning the Watter.*'—Done it twice : fell out of the boat, got nasty and wet, but thought it grand fun, though not *sport* !

Dynamite.—Saw it done in a Hungarian river once. Disgusting! Never desire to see it any more. Dastardly!

Night-fishing.—Done it often. Not keen on it. Cause of bad language.

Blue-bottle fly.—Used to practise this and kill, but gave it up in maturer years.

Creeper.—Ditto.

Diving minnow.—Ditto, and rather liked it.

Par-tail and minnow.—There is a phase of this which *is* sport, *i.e.* up-stream fishing with minnow. I am not an adept at it, but can realise that it is 'sport.' No doubt minnow is legitimate 'sport,' and 'par-tail' is a good bait for getting rid of rubbish, *i.e.* old big trout, which are cannibals with big teeth and do more harm in a stream than good, and ought to be killed at all seasons, as I think so should old black cocks and even old grey hens and old cock grouse all the year round.

Long ago, when our own home river was comparatively pure and held many fine trout, we used to go to the river-side armed with all the anglers' complete impedimenta. We had a trace mounted for spinning minnow

ready baited, and another for diving-minnow
ready baited, and one with worm all attached
to the under-side of our creel-lid, and a
strand or two round our hat ready for using
the 'nat'ral flee'—usually a big blue-bottle
or a large house-fly—and finally, a cast of
artificials attached to our line.   But we
were younger then, more patient than now,
and knew less; but our very keenness and
untiringness often resulted in our having
pretty bits of sport.   We would begin fishing
up a stream or a pool or a reach with fly,
then spin it down with minnow—we used a
somewhat stiff twelve-foot rod; then in the
dead reaches—time about, or as we found
best—a diving minnow or the natural fly,
and good fish were often taken thus.   Now,
however, we rarely practise these arts.
Somehow one's ideas of 'sport' change with
the years that go by.   Now we care little or
aught for anything but the artificial fly and
worm, and an occasional (very occasional)
fling with the 'birlin' mennen' (spinning
minnow) or the 'develin' mennen' (i.e. the
diving minnow) or the par-tail, but we do
not hanker after these methods.   As for fish-

ing out of a boat on the flat face of a loch, it won't compare with any wee bit mountain burn, and only as a change now and then do we practise it. Indeed, we rather dislike it than otherwise, though the day may come when one may 'needs be satisfied' to pump-handle away out of a boat.

Referring to Stewart's remarks as to the number of flies used by some fishermen, he says, 'some use a dozen.' This is, we believe, principally practised on the clear upper waters of the Clyde and Tweed. We have fished the Clyde but never happened to see the method in operation, so we are not in a position to speak accurately concerning it; but it finds its principal exponent and advocate in *The Angler and the Loop Rod*, by Mr. David Webster, who, as we are informed on the title-page, has been 'forty years a practitioner in this art.' In this book of Tweed and Clyde there is a most useful map of the upper reaches of these rivers, giving all the reaches on which the different winds blow *up* on Tweed and Clyde and their tributaries. Not knowing, we cannot say decidedly, but we think we would prefer to continue as we have formerly done with four

flies at most for medium and high waters,
and come down to two for low, clear, and
crystal. We practise three usually, at times
four, early in the season (when we then fish),
but should the water come below 'medium'
of scale and gauge, then we use two only, *not
far apart*. Indeed, we are of opinion that
two anglers of equal expertness in up-stream
fishing will not differ much in results in the
evening should one use three flies and the
other only two. The greater numbers of
trout, we believe, are killed by the tail-fly
and top-dropper; and if an intermediate
dropper kills better than the others, then it
ought not to be an intermediate, and the
sooner it is changed to one of the other
positions the better, or a second and even a
third put on. The object in using from nine
to twelve flies on a loop rod and line, we presume, is to present a choice of flies, and cast
a longer line in order to cover more water
across and up.

K

XIII

CLOSE TIMES FOR TROUT

MUCH in the preceding pages tend to a belief now becoming prominent among true sportsmen - anglers, that a close time is necessary if our river-trout are to be saved from destruction.

A close time has recently formed the principal object of a large meeting of Scottish anglers in Edinburgh and Glasgow, under the presidency of Sir Herbert Maxwell, Bart., whose interest in all such matters is a household word.

Such a close time, however, we believe, if it is to be effectual, must be suited to a large variety of circumstances, to innumerable conditions; to each river or group of rivers under their own climatal peculiarities; to variations in altitude, temperatures, and seasons.

Legislation on such topics is in itself often

a difficult and intricate matter, like all legislation which is subject to often ignorant and
blatant and unreasonable opposition. Often
also such legislation is rendered inoperative
and futile soon after the Acts are agreed to
and passed into law, because the means
taken to bring culprits to justice are ineffi-
cient and unsatisfactory, and hedged about
with innumerable difficulties in practice.

The extraordinary prices now asked and
paid for 'trout' in our large markets, especially in our large manufacturing towns, must
offer sore temptation to gangs of poachers,
who harry the water often at dead of night,
and are seldom, very seldom, brought to justice. We believe we do not exaggerate when
we say *tons* of trout are thus captured and sold
to dealers, especially in Aberdeen, Manchester,
Liverpool, Leicester, Bradford, and Hull.

In 1897 trout were priced at the current
markets in Aberdeen during April, and even
earlier, at 1s. 6d. per lb.; and during April 1898
were advertised at 1s. 10d. per lb. in the *Aberdeen Free Press*, and at 1s. 11d. in the *Scotsman*
about the same time. Sea-trout and brown
trout are usually sold mixed, and these prices

refer to such; but when sea-trout are sold by
themselves, they bring twopence or three-
pence more per pound.[1]   When it is remembered the sea-trout are so-called 'Finnochs,'
usually taken by rod and line at the tidal
portions of the east-coast rivers, but also,
it may be believed, with nets, where no nets
are legal, at a time when they are descending
the rivers to the sea, and not when ascending
the same, surely such are not other than
well-mended kelts, or fish not fully recovered
from their long residence in fresh water.
The smaller fish may be, and no doubt are,
fish which have not spawned, and therefore
have recovered flesh and muscle to some
extent by the time they reach the tidal
water, and no doubt rapidly recover after

[1] Besides, the market prices for small trout rule higher
than those for *big trout*, and this means a premium to
poachers, increasing facilities for them to poach *small*
streams; and as regards the future supplies of *salmo
fario* in Scotland, it is burning the candle at the wrong
end.   The prices quoted are under date September 3rd,
1898, for Tweed and Teviot, viz.: 'Small trout, 1s. 7d.
per lb.; large trout, 1s. 6d. per lb.'!   Surely common
sense in legislation should regulate such prices and sales,
as well as regulate the size of fish which are to be sale-
able from rivers, and the average weight only allowed,
and the premium should rather be upon the *big fish*.

they get amongst their natural salt or
brackish feeding-grounds. But we are
assured that oftentimes when so-called
sportsmen have returned from this tidal
fishing with 'heavy record baskets of sea-
trout,' let us say at the mouth of Dee or
Ythan, and are reported by the fishing jour-
nals from the reports from fishing quarters,
that often these fish were 'thrown out to the
pigs' as unfit for human food, only a few
picked out as being 'really in wonderful
condition'—and some people will always be
found to 'pick out the best bits of them'
and praise them! We have seen the same
thing often. We have shaken the lanky
things off our salmon-hooks when fishing
for salmon in a well-known Ross-shire river,
when we could have filled our panniers twice
over. And the same day we have seen an
angler, who knew no better, produce a trayful of sea-trout kelts, and, in his plenitude
of pride and generosity, offer us 'a dish
or two.' One thing certain, if he eat them
all himself, I guess he'd be sick! Nevertheless, our laws permit this wholesale
slaughter of fish unfit for food.

When midsummer is passed, and 'autumn tints are glowing,' then may the sportsman-angler expect to see a fresh run sea-trout in all the vigour and perfect beauty of his scales. But tell it not in sportsmen's ears who know better, that fresh run sea-trout are found in rivers in March and April, nor yet in May.[1] The descent of sea-trout takes place on the west coast later by a few weeks. On the east coast they descend well up to the 10th or 15th May, varying a little with the seasons. We have seen them 'smashing' all over the pools within a few feet of our legs, in company with salmon kelts, and even an odd fresh run 'fish,' and scores and scores of brown trout, all feeding eagerly and hungrily on March browns or early duns or red-spinners, as the case may be.

Returning to the subject of netting. Netting off and destroying hundredweights, nay, tons, of trout—mature, average, and young indiscriminately—must be a too terrible scourge upon any river. But if such operations were conducted under the eye of

[1] The heavy sea-trout which run in March and April up certain west-coast rivers, are not *early fish*, but the late fish of the previous year.

responsible parties, and the great big trouts which lie in the deep pools were taken out periodically, it is likely that *good* might follow, and the sporting average be maintained and the numbers even increased. These big trout are practically *vermin*, and ought to be killed systematically, just as old black cocks and old cock grouse should be thinned off, and we would even go so far as to say treated like pike at all times by those who would conduct the operations properly, and be licensed to do so. We would have no close time for pike in trout waters, nor for hoary old sinners of trout, that live only for evil, and not for good. And, though we know we will at once receive adverse opinion and criticism for saying so, should any one consider it worth while, we would not preserve kelts, *i.e.* kelted fish, salmon, or big trout, to the extent which our laws provide for. But if netting *is* to be done (permitted), then it ought to be done by responsible parties seeing it properly conducted, and all young fish, or fish under a certain size, according to the river, *returned* to the water. If we owned a salmon river, for instance, which we do not, we would be loath to preserve or spare the huge, ugly, long, lanky twenty-pound kelts, preferring, as we would always do, the sport to be obtained from smaller fish, and more of them. More real sport, we hold, can be got out of grilse and small salmon than from all the glory of killing a big fish.

Of course a cry, raucous and indignant, may probably come from 'those who go down to the sea' in boats, who often forget to lift the leaders on a Saturday night, and love to see a 'monster' on their fish-slabs, far away and above the real average of their native streams.

The above are *points* which we hold ought to have some consideration should new legislation (and action) be taken in regard to our Scottish streams. Our small spring fish are our most vigorous and best breeders, and ought to be encouraged, but the late autumn big fish, which spawn in the lower reaches of our rivers, often amongst mud, and lose half their ova, ought to be less encouraged than they are; and the same remark may be held, in our opinion, as applicable to large trout which are far *over* the average of their native streams.

XIV

NOTIONS, NOTES, AND ODDS AND ENDS

TROUT IN SHOALS

' My boatman on Loch Errochd, Perthshire, related to me one day lately that in August 1880 a Mr. Anderson and himself saw a distinct ripple upon the surface of the loch, extending over a considerable distance, during a dead calm. Upon closer inspection, they discovered that it was caused by a large shoal of trout feeding on the surface. The water at the time was covered with small brown gnats—my boatman described it—"until the water was brown with them." On casting a fly into their midst they—the trout—all rapidly disappeared, but shortly afterwards were seen a short distance off breaking the surface as before, and causing the appearance of a ripple.

'Now, coming home to-day, August 18, 1880, I witnessed the same appearance, but on a much smaller scale than above described, and I have often before witnessed something similar elsewhere, but I am not aware of special notice of it having been taken. In Sutherland, on a loch in Assynt, named Faerlochan, I have more than once seen a large shoal of trout at a certain point where the burn enters, and a big stone juts out from the shore. It seems almost certain, I think, that trout are gregarious to a very considerable extent. Will this in part account for the rapid "tids" or "rises" the angler often meets with in one bay or shore of a loch when no "rise" is "on" in another? Whether they are always gregarious in lochs or not is another question, but the shoals seen in Faerlochan and elsewhere seem to point to this.

'In rivers, however, a "tid" is often just as marked as in a loch, and here, I fancy, one must look for other reasons.

'On Lochleven trout are seen occasionally to be "on the rise" all over the loch, and on such an occasion the sight is most curious, and, when dead calm, most tantalising to the angler. At others trout seem to be "on the rise" only in certain bays or on certain drifts, and sometimes only opposite one end of a boat, and not at the other.

'Surely naturalists some day will discover *reasons* for these peculiarities if anglers would only keep regular notes. I think there must be reasons for these phenomena, either below the surface of the water or above it, whether connected directly with the distribution of a food-supply or distribution of the fish themselves, or other causes. I know char go in shoals. A friend and self killed eighteen one day in a short time on Loch Garry, besides trout.'

The above note was originally sent to *Land and Water* years ago, and since then we have had many later opportunities of witnessing similar phenomena. There can be scarcely any doubt that trout are gregarious, and that this is distinctly observable on still water of lakes or ponds. But it is more difficult to decide the fact in running streams. Still, we have often found that on one reach of water of a river, while one angler has been success-

ful and made a fair or even a good basket,
another equally good angler using precisely
similar flies has had scarcely a rise.   It seems
difficult to say with any degree of certainty
how far such experiences are due to simply a
local hatch-off of flies.   A river contains presumably a greater number of lies for trout,
at least a greater number of *specially* favourable lies for individual fish, than the more
even and less variable shallows of a loch.

SOME EFFECTS OF AN ABNORMAL SEASON

The independent study of separate branches
of natural history and science often reveals
many simple laws of nature binding all these
various branches together in a wonderful way
not before suspected.   We may instance this
in a somewhat marked manner during this
year of cold and abnormal summer and east
winds (1898).   Indeed, such an abnormal
state of the seasons often provides food for
the mind, and reveals, on account of con-
trasts, the laws of Nature, which succession
of normal seasons fails to do, because these
laws are not sufficiently accentuated.

It is little more than a year ago that a natural law was brought into notice by Sir John Murray of the *Challenger*—one of the natural results of the work of the *Medusa* in taking soundings and temperatures.—That law, shortly stated, is: During an on-shore wind the temperature of the surface-water is higher than during an off-shore wind. And the simple reason assigned by Dr. Murray is: Although the off-shore wind begins in comparatively shallow water, still the displacement of the surface-water makes room for colder strata of water below to rise to the surface and take its place. But in on-shore winds the surface-water alone is agitated, as the agitation has either commenced in deeper water, or has travelled far enough to become raised in temperature by the sun or contact with the air.[1]

In normal seasons our prevailing winds are westerly, but in 1898 east winds have prevailed. Therefore the waters of the west coast were abnormally cold as compared with other seasons.

[1] In long continuance of cold weather and absence of sun heat, no doubt this would come to be in a great measure neutralised.

In normal seasons the temperature of our west-coast waters is usually warmer than those of our east coast, because westerly winds—*on-shore* winds—further influenced by the warm Gulf Stream, bring up the temperatures.

In normal seasons the temperature of our east - coast waters, reversing the above arrangement, is colder than those of our west - coast waters, because normal winds, being westerly, are off-shore, and, as every one knows, there is no Gulf Stream influence in the North Sea, or very little to speak of.

An equable temperature is thus kept up by natural causes and effects, and, if modifications do occur, they only act as safety-valves and compensation balances to Nature.

In normal seasons a very patent modification may be found in the compensating temperatures of river water. Thus the colder snow-water, descending from the mountainous districts to the east coast, such as the Spey, Dee, Tay, and Tweed, etc., meeting with the colder area of the North Sea, allows a vigorous race of salmon to ascend at an early season of the year, which populate the rivers from

February on till December, if not, indeed, to
February again. The equable temperature
of fresh water, and the salt water which it
meets, more readily induces salmon to ascend.
On the other hand, on the west coast, rivers,
with rare exceptions, run rapidly to the sea
from high mountain ridges, becoming exces-
sively aerated in their passage, and, bearing
the same snow brae in their bosom, meet
with a much warmer ocean, fed by the limpid
waters of the Gulf Stream. Here the salmon
are later of ascending, the summer run of
fish, say, commencing in May, being the
representative of the spring run on the east
coast rivers. We know of few exceptions
amongst east-coast rivers in the earliness of
their runs of migratory fish, though we do
know of certain variations between some of
these, owing to local position and character,
and slight differences of their circumstances
inter se. On the west coast the few exceptions to what has been stated as regards the
lateness of the run of migratory fish are
exceptions which, by their unusually great
compensating phenomena, are enough to
account for these exceptions. The earliest

rivers on the west coast, known to us, are
the Lochy and the Awe, and, formerly, the
Gruinards. Their compensating qualities
are: length of courses, large reservoirs of
fresh-water lochs throughout their courses
and near their sources, rapidity of descent,
complete aeration, and consequent warmth,
more nearly assimilating to the sea lochs
which they meet, and thus causing the
equable temperature between fresh and salt
water which is so necessary before migratory
fish will ascend. This is not a statistical
paper, but the materials to prove the general
acting of this law are not wanting, but only
withheld. And questions about the comparative rates of speed and flow and aeration of
certain rivers of the east coast, as compared
with certain other rivers of the west coast, at
once suggest themselves; but we believe these
can be answered statistically by any one who
will take the trouble to collect and arrange
the materials which have from time to time
been published.

If this were done thoroughly by those having the knowledge, accurately formed by
many years' personal inspection of, and

intimate acquaintance with, each river in Scotland, or for such river or rivers as he has statistics upon, great service would result to our salmon legislation, and to the knowledge of the habits of this valuable fish.

Nor are migratory fish only affected by the abnormal state of the present season. It is well known on our west coast how late the fry of many sea-fish were of appearing in 1888. Thus the fry of coal-fish and lythe were far later of reaching the surface above the shoals, and of approaching shorewards. This was perfectly evident even to the most unobservant amateur sea-fishermen. Where fry, in normal seasons, abounded along shore, and were chased by coal-fish and lythe and other species below, and fed upon by the birds of the air above, that year fry seemed almost absent.

Another consequence of this state of affairs is somewhat curious to relate. Arctic terns approach their breeding-places first about the 12th May, in normal seasons, but do not repair to their selected nurseries till nearly a month later. They come simply the first time to prospect and see, as it were, for themselves if they could safely take up their usual habitations. During the interval between the 12th May, say, and the 12th June, these terns often keep out far from land, usually hovering and feeding over certain shoals, and resting, when gorged, on the surface of the water. Later in the year, however, the fry hatched, or hatching out, on these fishing-grounds and rising to the surface, within reach of the terns, get drifted shorewards by the normal, warmed west winds, joining the later hatches of fish, which are later of reaching the surface, having been deposited in the colder strata of water near the shore. Then the terns follow, and, by the time of their nesting, their food is all around them in abundance. Nothing perhaps was more noticeable in 1888 than the lateness of the terns in their arrival at their nesting colonies. We have even a record of half-developed embryos in terns' eggs as late as 3rd August on the west coast ; late enough, even though it may have been a second or third laying. We believe also that this may have much to do with the continuous changing of sites so noticeable in these species of birds.

The east wind, as every one knows, continued with scarcely any interruption all the
spring and summer, even into the autumn
months, over the whole surface of Scotland.

We might follow this subject further, having in our possession comparative statistics of
the movements of herring on our coasts, and
the movement of solan geese for a number
of years, carefully taken and tabulated; but
this we consider is a little beyond our present
purpose, which is simply to draw attention
to causes and effects, and to the matter of
the first sentence of this communication,
and thereby to point out how all branches
of science may, and no doubt are, equally
deserving of attention as correlated; and if
attention cannot in *all* cases be given to
them by the selfsame individual, at least they
deserve support and encouragement where
such can be pointed out or suggested.

FLAVOUR OF TROUT—HOW AFFECTED— INSTANCE

Formerly, and within our remembrance,
the trout of the river Carron, in Stirlingshire,
used to be excellent, esculent and succulent,

and pinky or creamy in colour of the flesh, but pollution of the river [1] by 1879 rendered them utterly unfit for food. This deterioration had been going on and becoming more and more pronounced for many years before that date. In 1880 a distinct improvement took place in this respect, since the river was purified by the action of the riparian proprietors in common law, and by the introduction of fresh yearlings from Howietoun. This purification and restocking of the water below the former sources of pollution had occupied several years in accomplishing, but alas! just as it was about to be crowned by success, the united action by the said riparian proprietors was broken up by the withdrawal from amongst their number of the principal, and action in consequence was permitted to lapse. It is now little better than a sewer.

ORIGIN OF SALMONIDÆ

As is well known, many little streams, scarcely bigger than ditches, and often having only courses of a few yards in length, and

[1] Caustic soda or soda-leys.

which communicate directly with the sea, contain abundance of small trout; and it is equally well known that others even quite close to these are troutless.   Mr. Hardy, of Old Cambus, relates that many such small streams between St. Abb's Head and Dunbar contain trout, although these streams are nearly dried up in summer (*in lit.*).

Below the Smoo Cave at Durness, in a small stream which issues from the cave and runs a course of some thirty to forty yards to the sea, there have been small trout as long as local memory can recall, but in a mile or two of river above the caves, into which it falls with a fall of about thirty feet or more, there were no trout whatever until they were *taken* up from the small bit of stream below the caves.   These introduced trout are lovely in colour, a bright line of most brilliant and converging scarlet sealing-wax-like spots running along the medial line.

The trout of Loch an Sgearrach, in the Goberneasgach deer-forest, retain the par-markings through the adult stages, but these markings fade after the fish are taken out of the water.   This locality is separated from the Hope river and the sea by a fall of sixty feet.

The trout of another very small circular pool of considerable depth, also in the Goberneasgach forest, grow to a large size, and show peculiar, high-humped backs, and are very game and powerful fish. This pool lies high up in the hills, and the stony stream which descends the steep hillside from it is often dry for long periods together.

We could give from our personal experiences an account of many more of these curious conditions existing among trout in isolated localities, but most of these were at one time communicated to Dr. Day while he was writing his volume on British Salmonidæ. We only instance a few.

DEFORMITIES AMONG TROUT

We may here simply refer to the papers published in the Royal Physical Society's *Proceedings* and *Annals of Scottish Natural History* by Dr. R. H. Traquair, upon several varieties of these peculiar deformities, much of the materials for which papers were obtained and supplied by ourselves.

Local varieties in colour of trout is an almost inexhaustible subject, dependent on many varying causes, concerning which we have many observations noted; but we cannot enter into any further treatment of them in this place.

DESCRIPTIONS OF WEATHERS FOR AN ANGLER'S VOCABULARY

Winds

Blustering down-stream.   'Fatal fur.'

'Bad hat'—*i.e.* a L. and B.'s brushed the wrong way, or against the nap, in relation to wind and surface of the water.

' Rough-tongued,' ' dirty-tongued,' ' scrofulous.'

' Criss-cross,' ' flawy,' ' daddin',' ' unsteady.'

Half-gale ' up' or ' down' or whole gale.

' Raging all round like a bull in a china shop.'

' Fluffy,' ' faint flaws.'

' Hurtling' down- or up-stream; ' scurrilous.'

' Gap o' May,' ' Gowk-storm,' ' Tchuchetstorm' (phonetical spelling).

Snow, hail, sleet, rain; ' ghastly.'

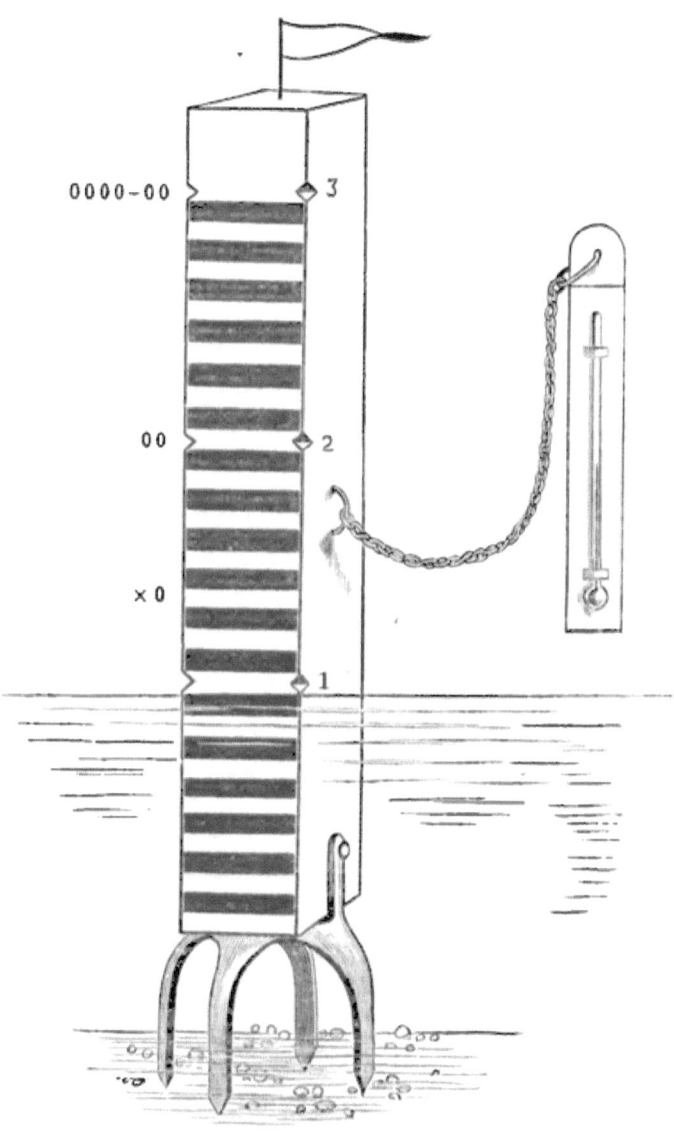

WATER-GAUGE.
(*Not to Scale.*)

WATER GAUGE AND DESCRIPTION OF STATES OF WATER

The gauge or scale is a stick or iron rod painted black and white in alternate inches, and driven into the bed of the stream when fairly low, and, say, three feet above water.

SCALE

0 0 0 0 – 0 0. Highest record, 1831 and 1829.

0 0 0 0 – 0. Next highest.

0 0 0 0. High-level floods.

0 0 0. High-level floods.

Any of above are unfishable. Yellow floods, pea-soup, clay, *may clear* to porter, peat, black, or even dark amber.

0 0. MEDIUM LEVELS

May be yellow, clay, but likely to clear through porter to amber ×. May run *milk*, *i.e.* snow-water. May be black or drumly.

× 0. LOW LEVELS FIRST TOUCHED

This should be a fixed point on gauge.

× 0. 0. [2].   Lower.   Clear.

× 0. 0. 0.   ,,   Crystal.

0. 0. 0. 0.   ,,

0. 0. 0. 0. [2].   ,,   Dead low.

0. 0. 0. 0. – [3].   ,,   Lowest records.

The three stages marked × are best, and amber of 0 0 –.

Stake driven down till *medium* mark is touched by water.

Skies

Dark, heavy, cold grey; inky, like blots on blotting paper; sky with clots of ink; no sun, 'woolpacks,' 'dark and light cumuli,' 'piling up round the horizon,' 'dense dark drift'; 'lurid,' 'threatening,' 'thundery,' 'electric,' 'sultry,' 'hard and cold,' 'compact and uniform black,' 'great black and inky rain-clouds'; foggy, misty, frosty, sultry, hard.

'Bright,' 'glittery,' 'glancing,' 'glaring,' 'blazing,' 'cloudless blue,' 'blue with cumuli,' 'fitful sun-shafts,' 'sickly gleams,' 'a blazer,' 'slight cloud-motion overhead,' 'brilling,' 'as hot as when hens jump up at flies.'

'Mackerel,' 'high drifting cirrus.'

'Roving,' 'warm blue,' 'hard blue,' 'balmy,' 'moist,' 'light and blue breaking through,' or 'light cloud and blue between,' 'high film and strata,' 'broken sky.'

Water

(See Table of Scales and Gauge.)

Flooded, 'yellow flood,' 'clay' (usually road and surface washings), 'ink,' 'high and dark,' 'drumly,' 'inky' (often due to sky reflections, at least in part), 'turbid' (much sediment moving).

Peat, porter, reddish brown, amber (dark or light), 'clearing,' 'golden.'

Clear, crystal.

'Fatal fur' (due to wind and sky colours combined).

Leaden (due to reflections).

Polished lead, dark steel, polished steel (the latter usually in bright sky with hard clouds and cold air).

'Coppery glare' (with lurid sky).

Green (reflections from trees or foliage or grass banks, usually an evening effect, but also at times during the day).

'Sullen,' 'sulky,' 'metallic,' 'bad hat,' 'rough tongue,' 'furred' (by the wind).

Weather

'Cold,' 'Cauld, cauld, cauld upon the lea; jist aboot as cauld as it can be'; 'some saft-like,' 'gey lowse-like' (*i.e. loose-like*, referring to rain expected); 'awfu' wather,' 'fair rideeklous' (as the meenister said, when praying for better weather, and it came on to rain 'waur than ever' : ''*Deed, Lord, it's fair rideeklus*')—Dean Ramsay.

'Camsteery' (*i.e.* unsettled : 'ae thing ae day, and anither anither day,' 'never twa days the same.'

'Maist dislogical wather.' (I only once heard this, and it stuck.)

'Drouthy' (*i.e.* 'some dry'); 'fine growin' wather' (*i.e.* warm, moist, genial).

'Raal intellectual wather.' (I heard this also off-hand, as descriptive of 'growin'' weather—opposite of 'dislogical.')

CONDY'S FLUID—PERMANGANATE OF POTASH

Mr. R. B. Marston, editor of the *Fishing Gazette*, has some interesting suggestions in that magazine (April 9, 1898) as regards the possible advantages of using permanganate of potash for clarifying ponds and tanks.

The action of this chemical ingredient is 'precipitation' of deleterious or other matter or solids in suspension.

It can hardly perhaps be considered exactly an equivalent for *aeration* of water, though the effect upon the fish might prove very similar.

FORMALINE

A warning is held out to anglers in a recent number of the *Fishing Gazette* (*loc. cit.*, April 23rd, 1898).

Prolonged use, it is said, may cause neurosis of the tissues of the nose and other serious evils.

Though the weak solution used for preserving minnows, or fish of all sorts, may be (and doubtless is) less likely to do harm than the stronger solution as sold by chemists, still the warning is not to be despised. One to two and a half per cent., we believe, is sufficient to preserve minnows for fishing purposes. The solution sold is, we believe, seventy-five per cent. of formaline.